OUR
HOUSE

TIME to SHINE

OUR HOUSE

TIME to SHINE

T. S. EASTON

Piccadilly
PRESS

First published in Great Britain in 2016 by
PICCADILLY PRESS
80–81 Wimpole St, London W1G 9RE
www.piccadillypress.co.uk

A CIP catalogue record for this book is available from the British
Library.

ISBN: 978-1-8481-2568-1
also available as an ebook

1

Typeset in Sabon 14pt Extended by
Palimpsest Book Production Ltd, Falkirk, Stirlingshire

Printed and bound by Clays Ltd, St Ives Plc

Piccadilly Press is an imprint of Bonnier Publishing Fiction,
a Bonnier Publishing company
www.bonnierpublishingfiction.co.uk
www.bonnierpublishing.co.uk

For Catherine

PART ONE
August

Fight, Fight!

I rushed into the tent just in time to see William D swing a tent pole at Uncle Ryan. He missed and fell over. Uncle Ryan took the opportunity to kick William D in the bottom. William D shrieked, sprang to his feet and leapt on top of Uncle Ryan, knocking him over. Daisy and I looked at each other in alarm and rushed forward to grab hold of our little brother and haul him away from the fight. Our cousin Brittany came running into the tent and took hold of Uncle Ryan. The two boys burst into tears.

William D has a love-hate relationship with our uncle. Ryan's favourite game is winding William D up. They fight loads whenever we spend time with the Cooper-Deals, but they have a lot of fun together as well, and if you try to keep them apart they bawl their eyes out. We'd been sharing a campsite with the Cooper-Deals for three days and, as Mummy put it, we'd all 'been on a bit of an emotional rollercoaster'. My friend Emily thinks it's hilarious that William D has an uncle who is only a few months older than William D is. I suppose it's even odder to think that I have an uncle who is five years younger than me. But that's just the way things are with the Cooper-Deals. They're complicated.

Here goes: Ryan's daddy is Grandpa Jim, who is also Daddy's daddy. Grandpa Jim doesn't look that old but Daddy says he is. He gets confused sometimes, and Brittany told me last year that when they were at Pizza Express he went to the loo and accidentally did his wee in the Dyson Airblade hand-dryer. He got divorced from Granny Hattie a few years ago and married Auntie Lisa. She isn't really my auntie, she's my step-grandmother, but it's easier to say auntie, especially as she's much younger than Grandpa Jim and doesn't look much like a granny. Grandpa Jim and Auntie Lisa had a baby six years ago and that was Ryan, who is my uncle and my Daddy's half-brother. They are the Deal part of the Cooper-Deals. Like I said, it's all a bit complicated.

'You should respect your uncle!' Mummy says to William D. But William D doesn't respect Uncle Ryan at all and poured water on his sleeping bag this morning, which is what led to the fight they were currently having. Ryan is one of those little boys who like to do awful things and then run away laughing.

'You say sorry, William D,' Daisy said.

'SORRY!' William D wailed.

'You say sorry, Ryan,' Brittany said.

'Sorry,' Ryan sniffed. The boys hugged each other and

we left, job done, and went back into our tent where the floor was covered in colouring pens and books. I sighed happily as I looked out through the flap, which was whipping gently in the breeze. It had been hot, but a few clouds had rolled over now and it was threatening to rain. I didn't mind that though. It was a relief to feel a bit of a breeze.

It's a really nice camping site. We've been to some horrible ones, like the one in Wales where the septic tank overflowed and the one in Chipping Camden where the field was full of cows that came into our site and ate all the rocket salad. But this one was perfect. There was a stream nearby, and good walks along the cliff, and a shop, and we were close to a village with a pub and a fish and chip shop.

The grown-ups were having a snooze because we'd all had a fish and chip lunch. We girls had been put in charge of keeping the boys quiet while they had a siesta, and if we managed to do that, our reward was going to be that we were allowed to go down to the stream on our own later. Daddy always insists on having a siesta when we're on holiday. 'We could learn a lot from the Europeans,' he says. 'They have the right work-life balance.' I flopped down on the mat where I'd left the medium-hard sudoku I'd been working on. Daisy sat down on a sleeping bag and got back to her drawing of a new Moshi Monster she'd invented. She was using my special Selecta pencils, the ones Granny Jean had got me for drawing wildlife. I didn't mind Daisy using them – we share everything. Brittany lay down right between us even though there wasn't really enough room.

'Do you like sudokus, then?' Brittany asked me. Brittany has a northern accent. All the Cooper-Deals do. I really like it but William D can't understand them sometimes.

'Yes,' I said. 'I find them relaxing.'

'Do you like them, Daisy?' Brittany asked.

'I've never done one,' Daisy said, peering over.

'Why don't you try one?' Brittany said.

'Can I, Chloe?' Daisy asked.

'Yes, when I've finished this one,' I said.

'You'll be ages,' Brittany said. 'Why don't you tear one of the pages out so Daisy can try it?'

'I don't like to tear the pages out,' I said shivering at the thought. 'I don't like to damage books.'

'But it's only a puzzle book,' Brittany said. 'You're writing in it, after all.'

'I just don't like doing it,' I said, feeling my cheeks get hot. Brittany can be a bit like Uncle Ryan sometimes. Just causing trouble for the fun of it. 'Why can't we just do what we were doing before?'

'Because Daisy wants to try a puzzle, don't you, Daisy?' Brittany said.

Daisy looked over at me. She knew how I felt about my sudoku puzzles. I was sure she would say no.

'Yes, I do,' Daisy said. 'Can I, Chloe?'

'Fine,' I said grumpily. I threw the book over but it hit her on the nose and she cried out. I told her to shut up or she'd wake the boys and she said she was going to tell Mummy and she stood up so then I stood up too and shouted at her that she mustn't wake Mummy because then we wouldn't be allowed to go to the river. Then she pushed me or maybe I pushed her and things got out of hand and Mummy came and shouted at us for waking her up. I was really cross with Daisy and glared at her. She glared right back.

When the fuss was over I noticed that Brittany was calmly lying on the mat reading a book. Brittany is almost exactly between Daisy and me in age and height and just about everything else. It's brilliant to have another girl around our age to play with when we see our cousins, but sometimes I think that maybe Brittany gets between me and Daisy in other ways too. Daisy and I don't argue much except when Brittany is around. I'm not really sure why or how it happens, but it always does. She just upsets the balance. As I calmed down, I realised it was silly to be cross with Daisy.

'Chloe, you apologise to your sister,' Mummy said.

'Soz,' I said.

'Don't woz,' she replied, and we grinned at each other. We never stay cross with each other for long. Mummy went back to bed and we got back to what we had been doing. But after a bit we heard more shouts from the

7

boys' tent, followed by a thump. We all had to rush in and pull Uncle Ryan and William D apart all over again. Babysitting is tough work.

Tash

As if the Cooper-Deal family isn't complicated enough, Auntie Lisa has a teenage daughter from another marriage. Her name is Natasha but she calls herself Tash. Her surname is Markham which is Auntie Lisa's maiden name. But we can't call our cousins the Cooper-Deal-Markhams because that's just getting silly. She's fifteen and wears black lipstick and doesn't smile much. Daddy says she's 'experimenting with emotions'; Mummy says she's sullen. The only time she ever smiles is when Jacob's around because she clearly adores him.

The next day, Tash and Jacob went out for a walk after lunch, while the grown-ups tried to have their siesta. Or at least Jacob had gone for a walk and Natasha followed him. I'd been teaching Daisy and Brittany about using Observation skills in the wild but we weren't allowed to go down to the woods on our own so we were just Observing things around the campsite.

So when Tash and Jacob came back we Observed them from the tent. Natasha lay on a blanket, sunbathing and chattering away to Jacob who was sitting on a tree trunk, texting someone and ignoring her.

9

'So how can you tell she likes him?' Daisy asked.

'Because as soon as they got back she rushed to her tent and changed into her bikini,' I said. 'And then she just happened to plop herself down next to him. It's just like the mating dance of the common house sparrow. Or rats.'

'She's just sunbathing,' Daisy said.

'It's spitting with rain,' I pointed out. 'She's going blue, not brown.'

'Also,' added Brittany, 'have you noticed how she keeps telling him they're not really cousins.'

'Why does that matter?' Daisy asked, mystified.

'Cousins can't snog, or get married,' Brittany said. 'My dad says lots of people in our town have married their cousins and it's not good.'

'Why not?'

'Because they might have babies with webbed feet,' I said. 'Like Puddleglum from *The Silver Chair*.'

'Or our postman,' Brittany added, before turning to me. 'Do you have a boyfriend?'

'No!' I cried.

'Does she, Daisy?'

Daisy shrugged. 'She likes Thomas.'

'I DO NOT!' I screeched, outraged.

'Shh,' Brittany said. 'You'll wake the grown-ups. Tell me about Thomas.'

My face grew hot. I know I blush easily and the problem is the more I think about it the redder I get.

Brittany is so annoying. I wish I could be like other girls, who never seem to blush. It must be nice to be able to mask your emotions.

'Don't be embarrassed . . .' Brittany went on but I shushed her as we heard Jacob's phone chime. It was 'Girl on Fire' by Alicia Keys.

Jacob has been getting a lot of texts while we've been camping. I had hoped they were mostly from Charlie, the girl who works in the chip shop back in Weyford and who Daisy and I really like. Jacob has been seeing quite a lot of her lately. Yesterday I asked Jacob if it was Charlie he was texting all the time and he said that was for him to know and for me to find out. He has different noises for different people who text, but I didn't know who was which. So I sneaked a look at his phone later, I had to be nifty to get to it before the screen locked. I saw that he'd had one or two texts from Charlie, but loads and loads from TABITHA. None of us liked Tabitha. She was flimsy and didn't brush her hair and never brought us presents like Charlie did. Jacob snatched the phone out of my hand before I could read any of the texts. But now at least I knew who was texting him. When it was Charlie, the phone would play 'Bang Bang' by Jessie J, and when it was Tabitha, it would play 'Girl on Fire'.

Jacob hadn't really wanted to come camping at all, but just before we left we got a tearful call from Auntie Moira. Auntie Moira is Daddy's sister, and she married

Uncle Desmond. Brittany is their daughter. They are the Cooper part of the Cooper-Deals. Really the Cooper-Deals are two families, but they live on the same street in Durham and have sort of merged into one. Anyway, Auntie Moira phoned Daddy and said Grandpa Jim was refusing to come if Auntie Lisa didn't come and Auntie Lisa couldn't come because Natasha had locked herself in her room and wouldn't come out. Mummy looked delighted and said 'let's just not go' because she doesn't like camping anyway but Daddy gave her a look and said he'd sort it all out. Auntie Moira thought that Tash might be persuaded to come camping if she knew Jacob would be there. So Jacob had sighed and agreed to the Family Deal on condition that we didn't go too far away from home and that he got some phone credit out of it.

Daddy had wanted to go all the way to Wales. He thinks if you're going to pack up the car with the tent and food and sleeping bags and sleeping mats and camping stoves and a million toys to keep William D occupied then you might as well go a long way away. Mummy doesn't see that at all.

'It doesn't make any difference whether we go to a campsite just down the road or one a hundred miles away,' she says. 'We still have to pack the car. But the good thing about being close is we can pop back to the house if we realise we've forgotten something. Or to have a shower.'

'If you can pop back home for a shower, what's the point of camping?' Daddy asks.

'Exactly!' Mummy says.

'We're supposed to be having an adventure,' Daddy says.

'Ooh! An adventure!' Mummy says, sarcastically. 'Maybe we should go to Smuggler's Top and solve mysteries.'

'Well if you had your way we'd go to Basingstoke Ring Road Caravan Park and eat kebabs!' he says.

Another thing they disagree on is whether you should be allowed to get takeaway when you're camping. Mummy says yes, absolutely, and Daddy says everything should be prepared from scratch and cooked over a wood fire by hand.

Last year Mummy organised an Ocado delivery to the campsite and Daddy didn't talk to her all day. Though I Observed that he did eat the cardamom-infused artichoke hearts in extra virgin olive oil Mummy had ordered. Everyone loves camping except Mummy. She gets very cold and wears her puffy coat all the time, even when she's sleeping. Also, William D doesn't sleep very well and keeps trying to climb into her sleeping bag, and Auntie Moira snores so Mummy doesn't get much sleep at all. She just lies awake all night listening to Auntie Moira and the sound of animals trying to get into the tent and imagines we're all about to be torn apart by wolves.

'Wear ear plugs,' Daddy suggests.

'How will I hear the wolves coming in to the tent if I wear ear plugs?' Mummy points out.

There aren't any wolves around of course, but there are badgers and I saw one on the second night we were here. Daddy woke me up and held his finger to his lips to stop me talking, then he took me out of the tent and pointed across the campsite to a dark corner, behind another tent. I couldn't see it at first, but then it moved and I saw its white stripy nose reflected in the moonlight. I gasped and Daddy's hand squeezed my shoulder gently. He understands how much I like watching animals.

Habitats

I do like watching animals and Observing their behaviour in their natural habitat. Humans are animals too, of course. And being closer to nature on a campsite is the best time to really understand what people are like. Especially at mealtimes. In the Stone Age, people would all live together in big family groups and share communal cooking facilities, just like we were doing. Though I don't think they had Pow Pow Extra Hot Chilli Sauce.

I can see Mummy isn't having the best time ever. Auntie Moira drives her potty. She's one of those people who always has to help whenever she sees someone doing something. Most people say 'do you need any help?' first, but Auntie Moira just pitches in and almost always makes a total mess of whatever is being done. Mummy likes to be left alone to get on with things. But Moira gets in the way – she knocks over the frying pan, she puts things away when Mummy needs to use them, she adds salt even when Mummy has already added salt and so on. Mummy tries to hide her frustration but because of my Observing skills I can tell it really winds her up. I don't think anyone else notices.

'Just sit down,' Mummy says. 'Relax!' But Auntie Moira can't. She can't bear to just sit and let someone else do something for her.

I like it best when Daddy tries to pour her a drink. She's so anxious to make it easier for him that she'll thrust her glass out rather than make him lean over but she wobbles it around so that he ends up spilling drink all over her hand, then she runs off, close to tears, to get a cloth to wipe it up and everyone shouts, 'Sit down, Moira, it's just a bit of squash.' Auntie Moira is quite tall, like Daddy, and has the same colour hair and eyes (blonde and green) but in almost every other aspect she's exactly the opposite of him. Daddy has no trouble at all sitting down and letting other people get on with their work. He is always very happy letting other people lean across the table to pour him a drink.

Uncle Desmond is Auntie Moira's husband. He's really funny. He calls everyone either Champ, or Chief. I think this is because he can never remember their real names. I spent ages trying to work out what made different people a Champ or a Chief, but I haven't figured it out yet. Sometimes, when he's had a glass of wine, he calls you Buddy which makes you feel special. Desmond is slightly shorter than Auntie Moira and is starting to lose his hair. He is always smiling and loves a bargain. He's always telling us about this great deal he's got on his mobile phone contract, or on his new car.

16

'Just changed mortgage providers,' he told Daddy last night. 'Got such a low rate that they're paying me!'

He loves gadgets and told Mummy about this box thing that you can plug into your telly.

'Plug it in, and you get any channel, anywhere in the world. Any box-set you want, any film, all there at the touch of a button. You get box-sets even before they're shown on the telly.'

'Really?' Mummy asked, doubtfully.

'No joke,' Desmond said. 'You know that new Deadly Assassin series? We were three episodes in before they'd finished filming it.'

The Cooper-Deals don't have a tent, they have a sort of pop-up caravan thing that Uncle Desmond got from a neighbour who was going to take it to the scrapyard.

'Told him I'd take it off his hands,' he said.

The caravan looks like a car trailer, until you get to the campsite. Then it opens up like a flower, with platforms to sleep on and all covered by tent canvas. It doesn't look as pretty as a flower though. Maybe a rusty and saggy flower. Mummy calls it the Carbuncle. But all seven of them sleep in there, somehow – Grandpa Jim, Auntie Lisa, Uncle Desmond, Auntie Moira, Brittany, Natasha and Uncle Ryan. They all snore, the Cooper-Deals. Even Uncle Ryan. When I got up in the night to see the badger, I could hear them all in there snoring away. It sounded like a small sawmill.

'How much did you pay for it?' Daddy had asked, kicking a tyre.

'He paid me!' Uncle Desmond said. 'Saved him the cost of having it towed.'

'Is it safe?' Daddy asked, wobbling one of the sleeping platforms.

'Yes, of course it's safe,' Desmond said. 'But don't do that.'

I like Auntie Lisa, Grandpa Jim's new wife. She has loads of tattoos. 'I had tattoos before they were fashionable,' she says. 'Now it's all body art and fancy calligraphy and tats that actually look all nice and that. This is a proper tattoo, look.' She showed us her calf, which had a skull with a snake coming out of the eye. It looked a bit stretched and faded. There was some writing under it which you couldn't read.

'What's that bit?' Daisy asked, pointing to some squiggles at the side.

'Varicose veins,' Auntie Lisa said. 'They're not part of the tattoo.'

'Where did you get it?' I asked.

'Ayia Napa,' she said. 'Or maybe Alicante. Not sure. Do remember it got infected, though.'

Auntie Lisa is small and thin with very brown freckly skin and long dark hair. She is what William D calls 'a steamer'. Mummy won't let her smoke anywhere near the children, so she sneaks off into the bushes and comes back smelling like the campfire. Then she grabs Uncle Ryan or William D, who gag as she tries to kiss them. But Auntie Lisa doesn't seem to notice. She loves children. The best thing about Auntie Lisa is when she reads us stories. We all squeeze into the Carbuncle and she reads chapter after chapter of *Danny the Champion of the World*, or *The Twits*, or *Harry Potter*.

Mummy and Daddy don't read to me any more but one of them will always read to William D every night and sometimes Daisy and I go and sit on the stairs and listen in. But they never read more than a chapter, even when William D begs them. They say it's too late and they've got a million things to do and it's time for lights out and William D is always disappointed. So are Daisy and I.

But Auntie Lisa will read for ages and ages, doing all the voices, which she always remembers perfectly. She even stands up on the sleeping platform and waves her arms about sometimes as the Carbuncle rocks and creaks alarmingly and Uncle Desmond shouts at her to 'sit down, you silly old woman'.

Group Shot

On the last day of the camping trip we got up early to go for a walk. As we all assembled in front of the tents, Mummy rushed off to find her camera so she could take a 'group shot' and everyone groaned. Every time more than two of us stand near each other for half a second Mummy rushes to get the camera so she can take a 'group shot' but it never quite works out because someone will always run off. Or someone else will be having a sulk in a tent and refuse to get in the picture, or Uncle Ryan will stamp on William D's foot and start another fight. If we do ever get enough people together for a photo, Brittany tries to stand between me and Daisy and Natasha always stands right next to Jacob and puts her arm around him and says things like, 'Should we scrunch up more?'

So off we went for our walk. We trotted through the dewy grass down to the clifftop and looked out through the haze over the English Channel. I could smell the sea, and wild garlic. Bees zigged and zagged among the late summer flowers. You could tell it was going to be another hot day, but just then it was still cool with a gentle sea breeze. It was perfect and I didn't want it to ever end.

We ambled along the path, William D and Ryan taking it in turns to complain about tired legs in between fighting each other. Eventually Daddy and Desmond decided to carry each of them on their respective shoulders, to stop them complaining, but also to stop one of them pushing the other off the cliff.

Daddy stopped to look out over the sea. He smiled happily, took a deep breath and closed his eyes. 'That breeze is coming all the way from Spain,' he said. 'I can smell the paella.'

We all stopped and sniffed the air.

'You're right,' Jacob said, looking surprised. 'I can smell meat cooking. Is that chorizo?'

'I can smell spices,' I said as we carried on walking. 'It's like Mummy's herb garden.'

But then we walked around a corner and saw Fat Harry's Snack Van in a seaside car park and realised that's what we'd been smelling. We stopped and got bacon sandwiches and sat on benches.

'Oh, so you won't let me get an Ocado delivery,' Mummy said to Daddy. 'But you're happy to eat bacon sandwiches from Fat Harry's Snack Van.'

'It's foraging,' Daddy said with his mouth full and melted butter coating his fingers. 'So it's allowed.'

The seagulls screeched at us as they soared around, watching carefully in case we dropped anything. But we didn't, it was all too yummy – the soft, white bread squashy with butter and brown sauce and the bacon all crispy and salty as the sea.

Even William D and Ryan stopped fighting for a bit and it was wonderful. Mummy had big sunglasses on the top half of her face and a big smile on the bottom half. As we ate, William D did one of his quizzes. He is going through a quiz phase. He'll ask you a random question and then gives you three multiple choice answers.

Some of them are really easy. Like 'Is the sky A) Blue B) Pink or C) Green?'

But sometimes they're a bit harder, like 'What is BattleTron's second Special Attack? A) Flame Ball B) Sonic Boom C) Lighting Strike.'

This is a question about BattleMasters, a game William D downloaded on Mummy's iPad. Daisy has played it so she sometimes gets the answers right but everyone else has to guess.

'Where is the golden key on level four of MechaWorld?' William D said as we set off again along the clifftop path. 'A) Behind the left door B) Behind the right door C) Behind the middle door.'

'Err, middle door,' Daddy said.

'Wrong!' said William D, pleased to have caught Daddy out. 'It's the right door.'

'I knew that,' Ryan said.

'No you didn't,' William D replied. 'You haven't even played BattleMasters.'

'Yes I have, I'm on level twenty-three.'

'There isn't even a level twenty-three!' William D shouted.

'It's a SECRET LEVEL!' Ryan screamed back in his face. Auntie Lisa grabbed him before the boys started fighting again and made him walk at the front of the crocodile. It was starting to get hot by then and to escape the sun we did a big loop back to the campsite through some pretty woods and stopped at a stream to have a rest and a play. It was so lovely and cool under the trees that we all decided to stay. Mummy and Auntie Moira went back to the camp to make a picnic and came back a bit later with a cool box full of sandwiches and drinks. Because it was the last day we had lots of random things to finish up so I had tuna and Branston Pickle. William D had ham and beef and salami. Daisy had cheese and egg.

Jacob went for a swim in the pool and Natasha sat on a rock nearby in her bikini pretending to read but actually just watching Jacob. I could see her flicking her hair occasionally to get his attention. We stayed for ages and only decided it was time to leave when we saw Uncle Ryan hurl an enormous rock at William D and nearly hit a child from another family.

'I'm in charge,' Ryan screamed. 'I'm your uncle.'

'I'm on the school council,' William D hollered back. 'That's higher than uncles.'

We got back to the campsite in the early afternoon and the grown-ups had a siesta while we played boules.

As evening approached, we had a last barbecue. The grown-ups all had beer and we were allowed to finish two big bottles of cola and we played Mrs Mumblegum and Mummy was so good at it – she kept a straight face throughout and Daddy was nearly sick with laughter. I could tell Mummy was really enjoying herself.

After a few rounds of Mrs Mumblegum, William D crawled onto Mummy's lap and Ryan crawled onto Auntie Lisa's lap. It was only eight o'clock but they were exhausted and they both went to sleep. As it got dark and the solar lights strung up around the gazebo started twinkling I thought just how perfect the whole day had been. Even though the Cooper-Deals could be a bit loud and were even madder than our family, they *were* family and I liked it when we all got on. It was the last day of camping and the last weekend of the summer holidays. On Monday we'd all be back at school. Year Six, my last year at Weyford. William D's last year at St Andrew's. But for now, there was nothing to think about except drinking cola and eating Pringles and arguing about whose turn it was at Mrs Mumblegum.

'So how's the house coming along?' Desmond asked Daddy when the game was finished.

'Err, slowly,' Daddy said. 'Have you not been to visit yet?'

'No,' Desmond said.

'I've only been once,' Grandpa Jim sniffed.

'You MUST come soon,' Mummy said.

'Just waiting for the invite,' Moira said with a face.

'It's just so difficult finding a time,' Mummy said.

I could see she was backpedalling a little now. I love this sort of Observation. Watching families and spotting clues that reveal how people are feeling and what they're really thinking as opposed to what they're saying. It's not easy. Humans are harder to read than any animal – except cats. Cats always surprise you.

'You should come at Christmas,' Daddy said.

'Yeah, we might just do that,' Moira said.

Mummy pursed her lips and looked like she was about to say something when Jacob's phone went off. A text alert – 'Bang Bang' by Jessie J. Charlie's tune. Jacob ignored it.

Maybe he was going to check it later, I thought.

CANOODLING

PART TWO
September

Back to School

We were all a bit down on Monday because the holidays were over and we'd had to get up SO EARLY. Part of me wanted to go back to school because I'd get to see all of my friends again. But at the same time I was a bit worried about it and hadn't slept very well. What if I didn't like my new classroom? What if the work was really hard? My friend Emily had told me that she'd heard you got TWICE as much homework in Year Six. Also, I'd be back in a class with Imogen Downing, my arch-enemy, who'd been sunning herself in Barbados for most of the holidays, plotting new ways to make me feel sad and small.

Daisy was nervous too. She'd had a lovely teacher in Year Three and didn't see why she had to move up to Year Four at all. If Daisy had her way, she'd never grow up. 'Why can't things just stay the way they are?' she often asks.

William D, on the other hand, was as chirpy as a sparrow. He had an inset day, or 'insect day', as he calls them. He was going to Little William's house for a play date while Mummy went to work. He was running a quiz over breakfast but none of us really wanted to join in.

'What type of animal does bacon come from?' he asked. 'A) Cows B) Chickens C) Goats.'

'D) Pigs,' Mummy replied. She was leaning against the Aga, sipping her coffee and frowning at a patch of damp wallpaper over the door. It was a little chilly that morning. Autumn was coming and the trees were looking as tired as we felt. Through the glass doors in the kitchen I could see dozens of apples that had fallen off the Bramley, half-hidden by the grass.

'No,' William D said. 'The answer is B) Chickens.'

Mummy sighed. I knew just how she felt.

Imogen was as brown as a cup of tea that's had the bag left in it too long. When I got to school all the girls were around her in the playground and listening to her go on about Barbados. Some of the boys were watching too, from a distance. I saw Thomas, and waved, but I don't think he saw me.

I had already met my new teacher, Mr Bolli, who runs the after-school Italian club as well as the Theatrical Society. We all love him because he uses his arms a lot when talking and gets really enthusiastic. He speaks English with a strong Italian accent and talks really fast, joining up his words so sometimes you can't understand what he's saying. He greeted everyone individually as we came in the door.

'GoodmorningaChloewelcometotheclassofSignorBolli!'

'Err, thank you,' I said, and giggled.

He is quite short and has wiry black hair that's thinning a bit on top and olive skin. When he saw Imogen he took a step back.

'You are Italian, no? You are so brown.'

Imogen gave him a look. 'I'm English,' she said. 'I've just been to Barbados.'

'Of course you have,' Mr Bolli said. And as she passed I saw him roll his eyes a little. I think he's the sort of person who finds it hard to mask what he is feeling. Just like me.

'This is your final year at Weyford,' Mr Bolli told us. 'And I am proud that you are in my class for this. You have a lot of work to do this year – there are exams to take next May. There is a residential trip to Montford. But first of all, and most important of all, there is the Christmas play. This year it is *Aladdin*: a very exciting story, full of love and danger and tears and laughter.'

As he said this, he held his hands to his chest and put on all these different emotions. Mr Bolli has a very expressive face and we all laughed. The Christmas play is always a huge deal at Weyford. Mr Bolli is one of the main teachers in charge. The other is the French teacher. She's a lady from Lyon who moved to England a few years ago and used to be called Mademoiselle Durain until she married Mr Adams who owns the bike shop and now her name is Madame Adams which Mummy thinks is the funniest thing in the world.

They try to get as many students as possible involved in the Christmas play. There's the band, and the set design, and the choir who sing between acts, and there are dozens and dozens of extras. Everyone packs into the school hall so there's not that much space left for the parents who come to watch. We have to do three performances to make sure everyone gets to see it. The speaking parts are mostly taken by the Year Sixes and some people take it very seriously. People like Imogen, who has been in every play since Year Three. Everyone expects her to get a lead role this year. Imogen has been taking private speech and drama lessons for years.

'She certainly is a drama queen,' Mummy says.

I wasn't really interested in the play. It's not that I'm scared about getting up in front of all those people, but when I auditioned in Year Three I was put at the back of the choir and in Year Four when we did *Cinderella* the only part I was allowed to play was a mouse and I didn't get a line. I didn't audition in Year Five and they put me in the band playing the kettle drum, which sounded brilliant until I realised that I only got to hit the thing three times in the whole show. I had to sit through six rehearsals and four performances including a matinee for hours and hours waiting for my bit. I started bringing something to read and I ended up missing the finale because of the exciting bit in an Alex Rider book.

So at first when Mr Bolli mentioned the play I didn't pay much attention.

'You might-a think that being in a play is not for you. You might-a think that it is only for the . . . *theatrical* people and acting is not something that will help you in your life. But you should think again maybe,' he said, tapping his forehead. 'Being in a play is the wonderful bonding experience. You will be working together, working hard, through thick and thin and it will bring you all together in camaraderie. You will develop respect and care for one another. Also, it is healthy to act in a play, to put yourself in someone else's shoes. To put on a mask and be someone else for a while. It builds confidence and empathy.'

I wasn't sure about the empathy bit, not if Imogen was anything to go by, but the confidence thing made me sit up. He was right. Acting was all about putting yourself in someone else's shoes. I think I'm pretty good at empathising with other people and guessing what they're thinking, but one thing I can't do is to put on a mask and pretend to be someone else. I would really like to be able to hide my feelings sometimes, like when Brittany is trying to wind me up, or Imogen is being rotten. I know people only do things to get a reaction from you, and if I could learn how to disguise my reactions, then maybe they'd leave me alone.

So at lunchtime I went straight up to the notice board outside the school office and wrote my name on the *Aladdin* audition list.

'You're going to audition?' Imogen said, appearing

behind me. I turned to see her standing with Meg and Sophie.

'Yes,' I said. It was time to try out my acting skills. Today I was going to be confident. I saw Thomas standing nearby holding a football. Oliver was talking to him, but he wasn't listening, he was looking over at us. At Imogen I suppose.

'Have you done any acting?' Imogen asked me.

'I've seen other people do it,' I said. 'It doesn't look very hard.' Well, Imogen got a furious look on her face when I said that and she wrote her name right under mine.

'Which part are you going to audition for?' she asked. 'The lamp?'

'I haven't decided yet,' I replied frostily. The truth is, I've never actually watched *Aladdin*, though I have read the book. William D has an old video tape of it in the playroom, though, and I decided I would watch it that night. Imogen was about to say something else when Thomas walked past us up to the notice board and wrote his name right under Imogen's. He didn't look at us, but turned away and ran after Oliver, who was already half way to the football pitch.

'Which parts are you going to audition for?' I asked Imogen as she walked away.

'Just Jasmine,' she said. 'I'm going to be Jasmine.'

It turns out Jasmine is the beautiful princess who Aladdin falls in love with. I don't remember her from the book. I think they might have changed it a bit for Hollywood. I was watching it on video in the sitting room when I heard a scream from upstairs.

Daisy and I ran up to find William D struggling to escape from under a huge sheet of wallpaper which had come away from the wall on the landing. Mummy clattered up the stairs and helped him out. We inspected the bare wall. It had black spots all over it.

'Mould,' Mummy said.

When Daddy came in from the garden, Mummy showed him the mouldy wall.

'It's not so bad,' he said. 'Makes quite a nice pattern, actually.'

'If there's mould, there's damp,' Mummy said. 'John, we need to get a proper decorator in and a builder to look at this.'

Daddy looked at me, clearly hoping I might help him out. 'You don't want new wallpaper do you, Chloe?' he asked. 'You wrote that report about the house and said you liked it just the way it is.'

'I don't remember writing *exactly* that . . .' I said.

'Chloe wants the same thing as me,' Mummy said firmly. 'Which is a top-to-toe redecoration of the whole house. Don't you, Chloe?'

'Well, maybe some new wallpaper might be nice,' I offered.

'We can't afford a complete redecoration,' Daddy said to Mummy. 'Maybe we could just paint over the top.

I'll go to Home 'n Garden Megastore on the weekend and get some tester pots.'

Mummy sighed.

As we were leaving class the next day I told Mr Bolli I had signed up for *Aladdin*.

'Fantastico!' he said. 'You will be brilliant.'

'I'm a bit worried about the audition though,' I said. 'I get a bit embarrassed. And when I get embarrassed I get tongue tied. I don't know if I'll be able to remember my lines.'

'Chloe,' he said. 'Don't-a worry. Even the best actors get nervous and forget their lines. Like Sophia Loren, she was terribly nervous.'

'Who?' I asked.

'Never mind. You want me to tell you a trick?'

'Yes please.'

'Are you any good at dancing?'

I shrugged. 'I used to do ballet. I was OK.'

'When you dance, if you practise enough, you remember the moves without even having to think. Right?'

'Right.'

'It's not like talking, where you can suddenly freeze and your mind goes blank. When you're dancing your body just keeps on going, even if you're nervous. OK?'

'OK,' I said.

'So think of each scene in the play like it's a dance,' he said. 'Tie your movements to your words. When you say the first line, you move like this,' he said, striding forwards. 'And when you say the next line you move like this.' He went up on his toes and put his hands behind his back. 'Then the next line you say while you clap your hands, then the next line you are turning around and pointing a finger.' As he spoke, he acted out all of the movements he was describing. 'You see what I mean? You teach your body to remember the moves and your mind will remember the words automatically.'

I looked at him sceptically. 'Does that really work?'

'It worked for Sophia Loren,' he said.

I think I need to find out more about Sophia Loren.

Mr Peterson

On Monday, when we got home from school, there was a man in the kitchen, sipping a cup of tea. He looked worried and had a pencil behind his ear. Daddy was there too and looked even more worried.

'This is Mr Peterson,' Mummy told us. 'He's a builder AND a decorator and he's come to look at the house to see how much it all might cost to decorate it. And rebuild it, perhaps.'

Daddy sighed at Mummy's 'joke'.

'Right, well you'd better show me this mould,' Mr Peterson said. We all trooped off towards the stairs. On the way, Mr Peterson stopped to look at the little patches of paint Mummy had been applying all over the hallway from the tester pots we bring back from Home 'n Garden Megastore. She adds two or three a week to the green-patterned wallpaper that was there when we moved in and writes the name of the paint at the bottom of each patch. They all look quite similar to me.

Mr Peterson peered at a couple. 'Jurassic Pebble,' he read. 'Wintergarden Hush . . . Snowflake Whimsy.'

He turned to look at Mummy. 'Have you decided which one you want to go for?'

'Not yet,' she said. 'But I'm getting closer. I can feel it.'

Mummy led the way up the stairs, followed by Mr Peterson, then William D, then me and Daisy and finally Daddy, who didn't really look like he wanted to be there at all.

I could tell Mummy didn't really want us following them around either, but we did anyway because we didn't want to miss out on the fun. I was glad we did. When Mr Peterson saw the flappy wallpaper and the mould on the first floor landing, he made a noise with his teeth, a sort of sucking noise. As we went up the stairs to the next floor, he pointed with his pencil to a couple of missing bannisters and made the sucky-teeth noise again.

'Why's he making that noise?' Daisy asked.

'That's the EXPENSIVE noise,' Daddy explained. 'The more times he makes that noise, the more money it will cost.'

On the second floor landing, the wallpaper and the damp were even worse. Outside Daisy's room, there was a huge section where all the wallpaper had come off altogether and there were great dark spots. It looked like a giant mural of *101 Dalmatians*.

Mummy showed Mr Peterson the bulging wall in the spare room and he shook his head.

'This isn't original,' he said. 'This partition's been put in more recently. Looks like the work of cowboys.'

William D's ears pricked up at this piece of information. I knew Mr Peterson meant cowboy builders, who were builders who did a rubbish job, took their money and ran off. I knew that because I sometimes watch *Extreme Cowboy Builders* with Daddy on MORE TV.

It was gloomy outside and the spare room is quite dark at the best of times because of the tree just outside the window. Mr Peterson switched on the light. It came on, flickered and went out with a pop. Mr Peterson sucked air again. Daddy groaned. The electrics were even worse on the third floor, outside my room. There were some wires actually coming out of a hole in the wall. Mr Peterson inspected them, poked the cluster with his pencil and sucked his teeth again before making a note.

'When was your last electrical inspection?' he asked Daddy. Daddy shrugged and Mummy shouldered him out the way.

'Not since the survey when we bought the house,' she said. 'Nearly three years ago.'

'You had a survey and they didn't pick this up?' he said.

'My husband arranged the survey,' Mummy said.

Daddy looked at his shoes.

'This is potentially dangerous,' Mr Peterson explained. 'Look, there's an exposed wire here.'

Daddy and Mummy exchanged worried glances but didn't reply. The wind blew outside and the squeaking started up.

'What's that squeaking?' Mr Peterson asked.

The squeaking is something that has been going on for a while; every time it's windy the squeaking starts and we can never find the source. It's not the bats, I know that. But what is it?

'We thought maybe you could find out,' Mummy said. 'It's driving us mad.'

Mr Peterson looked at Mummy and Daddy and shook his head. Like Mr Bolli did today when I forgot how to do fractions. Then he sucked his teeth again and I could tell Daddy couldn't take it any more – he went downstairs to put the kettle on and didn't appear again until Mr Peterson had left.

Later on, I took the script for *Aladdin* from my bag and read through it. The auditions were on Thursday at lunchtime so there wasn't much time to practise. There were two parts that really stood out for me. One was Jasmine, who had a lot of lines and was in most of the scenes. The other was the Grand Vizier, who had some funny lines and was the most interesting character. I wasn't really interested in being Aladdin because he is all brooding and heroic and never says anything funny. And also in the film he has his shirt undone.

When Daisy sings to herself and dresses up she stands in front of the mirror, so I did the same as I read out the lines for each character. I found being the wicked Vizier much easier than being the beautiful princess. Once

41

I had the cackle right, that is. Clearly the key to the role of the Vizier is the cackle.

Mummy came in at one point. 'What's that odd noise you're making?' she asked.

'I'm rehearsing,' I said. 'That's my cackle.'

'I thought you were choking,' she said. I read out some lines to her and asked if she thought I should try for the Grand Vizier or Jasmine.

'I'm not sure I'd make a very good Jasmine,' I said.

'Why not?'

'Because I'm not very girly,' I said. 'Imogen's much prettier than me, she'll definitely get the role.'

Mummy looked surprised. 'Firstly, no she's not. You are very pretty indeed. Secondly, how you look isn't important. At all. Thirdly, if you want to be Jasmine, then you should go for it. Never mind about Imogen.'

I felt better after that and made sure I learned the bits you needed to learn for the auditions. For Jasmine AND the Grand Vizier. Daisy came in and helped by reading out the other parts. She is really good at acting and performing, and I told her she should audition too, but she just shrugged and didn't say anything.

Audition

On Thursday, when Mummy was getting our bags ready for school she found a letter in Daisy's school bag. 'What's this?' she asked. 'Sex education class? This again?'

William D and I rushed over to read the letter.

Mummy has to go to an information session at the school next week so the parents can all watch the sex DVD before the children do and discuss what Daisy is going to be told about. I had to watch the DVD two years ago and it's all cartoons with hairy grown-ups and is a bit weird and terrifying. The boys all thought it was hilarious.

'I don't think Daisy is ready for this,' I said.

'I already know it anyway,' Daisy said. 'Brittany told me all about it.'

'All about what?' Mummy asked.

'You know. Snogging and affairs?'

Mummy sighed. 'This DVD hasn't come a moment too soon.'

The auditions were at lunch. I stood in the wings, watching as everyone went up and read their lines.

Some were better than others. Oliver just stared at his feet and mumbled. He was trying for the part of Aladdin along with Ben Ollerenshaw, Indren Patel and Thomas. Indren was very good and quite natural. But Thomas was the best, of course. Sophie was very funny and loud. Imogen was good and people clapped even though you weren't really supposed to but I think she overdid it a bit. She wore a veil 'to get into character' and did look very pretty with her brown skin, I had to admit.

Daisy had refused to audition for a speaking part but Tamsin and I had persuaded her to put her name down for a non-speaking part. She sat in the audience, watching, and it was good to know she was there. Then after what seemed like for ever, it was my turn and I shuffled onto the stage, my heart pounding. A spotlight came on and shone right at me, nearly blinding me, and I swallowed nervously.

'Tamsin, could you please turn off the spotlight?' Mr Bolli called. 'I don't think we need that right now.'

Tamsin was helping out. She really wants to be part of the stage crew, mostly I think so she can climb up ladders and dangle from gantries and that sort of thing. Tamsin is Daisy's best friend. She and I are kindred spirits because we both have lots of accidents. Tamsin specialises in falling off things whilst I'm better at dropping things that smash. We're both pretty good at tripping over and bruising our knees.

'SORRY!' Tamsin called from offstage and the light went off. 'Ow! That's hot.'

I could see Mr Bolli and Madame Adams now. They sat in seats a few rows back each holding a clipboard.

'When you're ready,' Mr Bolli called.

I'd decided to start by being the Grand Vizier because I found it easier to get into the character. Mummy had told me pantomimes were all about getting the audience to respond. The hero had to get a cheer. The villain had to get a boo whenever he or she came on stage. I decided if I was going to be the villain I was going to get the biggest boo ever. So I started with a hiss. Remembering what Mr Bolli had said, I was going to clap my hands at the same time so I had an action to go with the line.

I hissed. I clapped, and I had begun.

'Who is this boy ALADDIN?' I shrieked, striding forward. 'Who dares to threaten my power? I shall ruin him. I shall have him locked in the deepest dungeon.' As I said this, I moved across the stage, stalking like a praying mantis I'd seen on a nature documentary. 'The beautiful Princess Jasmine shall be mine,' I hissed, holding my hands to my heart. 'And when the Caliph dies, I will rule the empire.' As I said this last line I raised a fist triumphantly. Mr Bolli's trick had worked!

At this point in the play Aladdin and the genie are supposed to come on stage, but this was just an audition so I had to pretend I could hear them. I held my hand to my ear and opened my eyes wide in surprise.

'But wait. My enemy approaches. I am not yet ready to strike. I must bide my time.' I walked backwards off the stage, just like I'd practised. Unfortunately someone, probably Tamsin, had put a microphone stand in the wings. As I left the stage I fell over it and crashed to the stage floor.

'Bother,' I said. Just when things had been going quite well. Maybe they hadn't seen that. Thomas rushed over and helped me to my feet.

'Are you OK?' he asked.

'Fine thanks,' I mumbled, looking anywhere but at his face and feeling particularly embarrassed that he'd been there to see me make a fool of myself. I dusted myself off and came back out on stage.

'Thank you, Chloe,' Madame Adams said. I could see she was trying not to laugh and I felt my face go red. 'Now are you going to try for Jasmine too?'

'Yes,' I said, determined. I took a deep breath, relaxed and went all floppy, like I imagined a girly princess would be.

'Oh, Aladdin,' I began in a high-pitched voice. 'The Vizier's men are approaching. We are trapped. However can we escape?'

I turned to the empty space where Aladdin would be and fluttered my eyelashes as Mr Bolli read out Aladdin's line.

'Do not fear, sweet Jasmine,' he said. In the wings, I could see Imogen and Hannah watching me and whispering together. Imogen smirked and said something and Hannah looked up at me and laughed. I felt my face grow hot and I glared at them.

'Chloe?' Mr Bolli was saying.

'Oh, what?'

'Have you forgotten your line? It's "Oh Aladdin. I will marry you. But first we must flee!"'

I took a deep breath. 'Oh Aladdin, I will flee you, but first we must marry . . .' I tailed off and my heart sank. I'd fluffed my chances, firstly by falling over, than letting myself be distracted by Imogen and messing up the line. Why do I let her get to me like that?

I said the line and stomped off the stage, angry at myself.

'We'll let you know,' Mr Bolli said as I left.

Awkward

It had been so long since the last Date Night that when the doorbell went at 7.45 p.m. on Friday night we just looked at each other. Before the holidays, pretty much every Friday a girl would come to our house to collect Jacob and go out on a date with him. Back when he was irresponsible and immature he'd have dates with lots of different girls, but in the second half of the summer he started mainly going out with Chip Shop Charlie.

Charlie doesn't play by normal rules, which I love. She turns up whenever she likes, or sometimes she tells Jacob to pick *her* up or to meet her at the cinema. So our family tradition of interrogating girls in a sitting room filled with clouds of perfume and floaty scarves and too much make-up had ended. That was the only downside of 'Charcob', as Daisy called them. So anyway, that's why we were a bit surprised.

The bell rang for a second time.

'Can you get that?!' Mummy called from upstairs.

I walked down the hall, eyeing Front Door suspiciously. Front Door has a mind of her own and only seems to open when it suits her. Though she has been a little

48

more co-operative lately and opens two out of three times, I'd say.

'Hold on,' I called out to the visitor. I grabbed the knob and yanked hard and fast, which is the best technique, like you're catching Front Door by surprise. Front Door opened easily today and I realised I'd pulled a bit hard when I stumbled backwards and landed on my bottom. I looked up to see a girl standing on the top step.

'Charlie!' I said. I got to my feet and gave her a hug as Daisy and William D came clattering down the hall.

'Hello, you lot,' Charlie said, giving us one of her big smiles. She was wearing old jeans and a T-shirt and didn't seem to have made much of an effort. But she had brought presents for us all; models made out of those little wooden forks you get in chip shops. Charlie is very creative. She'd made William D a robot, Daisy a flower and for me she'd made a little cat. She knows us very well.

'I'll get Jacob,' Daisy said, heading for the stairs.

'I'll go. I'll go!' William D screeched, racing for the stairs and trying to trip Daisy up.

'I'm not here for Jacob,' Charlie said.

'Then why are you here?' I asked.

'She's babysitting,' Mummy said, coming downstairs and fiddling with one of her earrings.

Daisy stared at her, open-mouthed. Sometimes you can forget that Mummy is very pretty. When she gets all dressed up people pay a lot more attention to her. Like Imogen's daddy did after Christingle last year when he kept guiding her towards the mistletoe in Café Rouge.

'Yay!' I said.

'Are you going to play Bananagrams with us?' Daisy asked. 'Or are you just going to canoodle with Jacob in the sitting room, like the last babysitter did?'

'What?!' Mummy asked.

'I don't know what Jacob's doing,' Charlie said. 'I haven't heard from him for a while. I'm fully committed to Bananagrams for as long as is required.' She went into the sitting room and sat on the sofa.

'What's this about Jacob and the last babysitter?' Mummy asked as Daddy came downstairs, looking very handsome. He was wearing aftershave.

'Where are you going?' William D asked. 'Mummy, where are you g–'

'We're going to Vicky Bellamy's for a dinner party,' Mummy said, distracted. 'And what do you know about canoodling anyway, Daisy?'

'I don't see why we need a babysitter,' Daddy whispered so Charlie couldn't hear. 'We're only going over the road.'

'You know why we need a babysitter,' Mummy whispered back. 'Remember the hair curler incident?'

We all looked over at the burn on the sitting room carpet and Daisy went red.

'Come on,' Daddy said. 'We're late.' He ushered Mummy out of the door. She was still asking about Jacob and the babysitter as they disappeared into the autumn night.

Charlie looked at us, clapped her hands together and said, 'Let's Bananagram!'

William D insisted on playing, which spoils things a bit. He doesn't know how to spell many words and always tries to put down rude ones. This time though, Charlie was in charge of the scoring and gave him extra points for rude words even if he spelled them wrong, like *pu* and *botum*.

After a bit he got bored and went off to watch a My Little Pony video and we decided to play Junior Scrabble instead. At around 8.15 p.m, the doorbell rang again. Daisy got up but Charlie put a hand on her shoulder lightly.

'I'd better go,' she said. We all followed anyway and watched as Charlie tried, and failed, to open Front Door.

'There's a technique,' I said.

Charlie dropped to her knees and peered through the letter box.

'Tell the person to calm down,' William D, who had come out to investigate, suggested.

'Hello,' Charlie said. 'I'm afraid the door's stuck.'

There was a pause. Then someone outside, a girl, said, 'Charlie?'

'Hello, yes. Who's that?'

'It's Tabitha.'

There was another pause.

'Awkward,' William D said.

Triangle (Part One)

Tabitha was looking at Charlie.

Charlie was looking at Jacob.

Jacob was looking backwards and forwards between Charlie and Tabitha.

Daisy was looking at me. I think she thought I might be able to sort everything out.

William D was looking at Tabitha's hair, which was pretty messy, even by her standards.

I was looking at all of them.

Charlie had helped Tabitha in through the sitting room window while William D went up to get Jacob. Tabitha was wearing a crop top and short shorts over black tights. She had a ring in her belly button.

'What's that on your wrist?' William D said to Tabitha, breaking the silence.

Tabitha showed him her wrist. There was a tattoo of a little rose, black and red. We all peered at it. It was nicer than Auntie Lisa's skull tattoo.

'What's your tattoo say?' Tabitha asked, pointing at Charlie's hand.

Charlie looked down. 'It says "buy milk",' she replied. 'It's just biro.'

'Why is she here?' Tabitha asked Jacob, still looking at Charlie.

'I'm babysitting,' Charlie explained.

Tabitha looked over at us as if she'd only just noticed we were there.

'Sorry about this,' Jacob said to Charlie. 'This is kind of awkward.'

'Uh-huh,' agreed William D.

'Not at all,' Charlie said, smiling. 'Why should it be awkward?'

'Yes, why should it be awkward?' Tabitha added. 'You and I are going to the club, Carly is babysitting these children.'

'Charlie,' I said. 'Her name is Charlie.'

'Of course. How could I forget Chip Shop Charlie?' Tabitha said. She gave Charlie the sort of smile that Imogen sometimes gives me when she's pretending to be nice.

Jacob hurried Tabitha out through the window after that and we went back to the kitchen to carry on our game of Scrabble. Charlie kept on smiling but I watched her closely and I could tell she was cross and upset.

'I thought you were Jacob's girlfriend,' Daisy said.

'Apparently not,' Charlie replied, putting down the word L-O-S-E-R on the Scrabble board.

Something had clearly happened between Charlie and Jacob. But when? And why? Charlie is AMAZING and she obviously thought Jacob was too, so what was he doing going out with silly old Tabitha? Daisy looked a bit upset.

'We don't like Tabitha,' I said.

Daisy shook her head. 'No we don't,' she said.

'I'm sure she has her good points,' Charlie said, putting down C-O-W even though it wasn't her turn.

Milk Run

The next Wednesday I woke up early. It was freezing. I love my little room at the top of the house, but it does get very cold up there in the winter. The radiator is tiny and doesn't work very well. I don't want to complain about it though, because Mummy will just insist I move into the bigger room on the next floor down that's supposed to be mine. It has a Megadeath mural on the wall. The radiator in there is huge and boiling hot and you can't turn it down. Daddy calls it Sizewell B which is his little joke because that's the name of a nuclear power station.

Sometimes I wake in the night and I can see my breath in the moonlight that sneaks in through the thin curtains. I stick my head under the duvet and after a bit my breath warms me up again until I run out of breath. Then I pop my head back out into the cold again. I call this procedure 'ovenning'. Anyway, today there wasn't time for ovenning, I had a more important task to accomplish. I leapt out of bed and quickly put my slippers on. I scuttled downstairs and out through the sitting room window to see Cara. I didn't bother with Front Door because it had been raining overnight. Even if she opens she makes a lot of noise, scraping and creaking and whatnot, especially when it's been raining.

Cara is our milk lady and my friend. Sometimes I wake early and go and help her with delivering milk up and down our street. I'm not sure if I'm that much help, to be honest, because I sometimes drop milk bottles and smash them on the pavement. Also, one time, when Cara was delivering grapefruit juice to Mr and Mrs Simpson and left me alone on the float, I accidentally took the brake off and the float crashed into a bollard.

At first I didn't tell Mummy and Daddy about helping Cara, but then she came to the party we had in the summer and I introduced them because it all would have come out in the end. Mummy was a bit cross with me for leaving the house on my own and going off with 'a stranger'.

'She's not a stranger,' I said. 'She's my friend and she's lovely.'

So Mummy gave me permission to help Cara once a week, on Wednesdays, and that arrangement worked best for everyone. Cara is always on schedule and as I ran down the stairs I heard the hum of the electric milk float turning into York Road.

'Morning,' I whispered.

'Morning,' she whispered.

An owl hooted as I hopped into my warm seat and Cara and I grinned at each other. Cara has a new milk float that she's very proud of. The new float has under-seat heaters which blow out warm air against the back of your legs as well as warming the seat itself. It also has sat-nav but Cara doesn't use that because she doesn't need it.

'So what's new?' I asked.

'Around here? Not much. Except Mr Campbell had to go into hospital for a week. He stopped his milk. Oh, and the Fishers have his mother over to stay. She plays cribbage. They're getting an extra carton of eggs and pineapple juice.'

'How do you know it's Mr Fisher's mother and not *Mrs* Fisher's mother? Or someone else altogether?' I asked. 'And how do you know about the cribbage?'

'I've been doing this a long time,' Cara answered mysteriously. 'You get to know people very well through the little notes they stick in the top of milk bottles.'

She pulled over so I could hop out and deliver two pints of skimmed milk to the Fowler house.

'So what was unusual about that order?' Cara asked when I got back.

I thought for a bit. I'm quite good at noticing things. Nature, people's emotions. But what did I know about milk?

'They normally take semi-skimmed,' I said after a while.

'One semi for her and one full fat for him,' Cara corrected. 'She's on a diet. And she's put the rest of the house on a diet too. He won't be happy about it.'

Cara didn't sound happy about it either. She's told me before she doesn't approve of skimmed milk. 'It's disrespectful to the cow,' she says.

I told Cara about the play and how I'd auditioned for the part of Grand Vizier and also Jasmine.

'You'll be brilliant whatever you do,' Cara said. 'I was in a school play once. *Oliver.*'

'What part did you play?'

'I was a street urchin,' she said with a sigh. 'I wanted to be Nancy. But Jane Kingston got that, she was pretty with long red hair.' She paused as she got out to make a delivery and in the still morning air I heard the rumbling swoosh of a train passing through Weyford station. The seat heater was keeping me cosy and warm and I yawned happily.

'You're pretty too,' I said when Cara came back. 'You would have been a brilliant Nancy.'

'I know,' Cara said. 'Which part would you rather have in your play?'

'Well, I think I'd be best as the Vizier,' I said. 'And he gets loads of great lines. But I'd quite like to get the part of Jasmine. Imogen thinks she's got the part so I'd quite like to beat her.'

'Imogen's your Jane Kingston,' Cara said, stopping the float outside Mr Campbell's house.

'Yes, she is,' I said. It was my turn to make a delivery but Cara put a hand on my arm to stop me getting out for a moment.

'Just ask yourself this – what's more important to you; beating Imogen, or getting the part you want?'

Act One

On Wednesday in English Mr Bolli taught us about how to write a script, for a play or a movie or a TV show. Part of our homework this term is to write some scenes from a drama.

'But this is a show about you and-a your life,' he said. 'To describe your house and family, but you do it as a script, yes? Like from a play or a movie or a TV show.'

Then Mr Bolli went on to describe how we were to do it. He said we should choose a typical scene from our ordinary life but maybe jazz it up a bit. Then use stage directions and dialogue to tell the story. It sounds really cool. Here are some of the terms we learned:

Int: Interior
Ext: Exterior
CU: Close up
FX: Special effects
SFX: Sound effects

*   *   *

I'm really excited about it. I love writing and Observing and so this is right up my street. I decided I was going to write a screenplay about the next interesting thing that happened in our house.

I didn't imagine I'd have to wait long.

Head Hunters!

After school that day we played in the garden for a bit as the weather was quite warm. Mummy even came out for a while with a cup of coffee and a magazine, though she didn't get much of a chance to read it because William D came and sat on her lap and snuggled up to her.

'You're like a lovely wobbly whale,' he said.

I knew he meant this as a compliment. He loves sea creatures and calling someone a whale is about the nicest thing he can think of. But I'm not sure Mummy appreciated it.

'That's not a very nice thing to call a lady,' she said. 'Whales are quite large, you see.'

William D realised his mistake and corrected himself. 'Err, I meant you're like a lovely wobbly walrus.'

'Thanks,' Mummy said. 'That's much better.'

'Daddy!' Daisy cried as he appeared around the side of the house. 'You're home early!'

We all leapt on him and he tumbled over laughing. Mummy made him a cup of tea and we all had cake and he told us about his day. It turns out Daddy is looking for a new job. He told us he has sent his details to a firm of head hunters.

William D's eyes bulged. 'I want to be a head hunter when I grow up,' he said.

'It's not like it sounds,' Daddy explained. 'A head hunter is someone who tries to find people who are perfect for a particular job.'

'They haven't hunted your head though,' I pointed out. 'You sent your head to them.'

'For a big enough pay rise,' said Daddy, 'they can have all of me, not just my head.'

'What about the job you have now?' Daisy asked. 'Don't you like it?'

'I don't mind the job,' Daddy said. 'But it doesn't really pay enough money. Also I don't like commuting up to London. Sitting in that crowded carriage with the same people every day. There's a man who always sits opposite me who's a sniffer. Only in the winter, mind, but it's coming. As soon as November comes around, he'll get a cold, and start sniffing. Very loudly, and every minute or so. Like clockwork. Sniff . . . sniff . . . sniff . . .'

'Doesn't he have a handkerchief?' I asked.

Daddy shook his head. 'No he doesn't,' he said. 'He doesn't have a handkerchief. Why wouldn't a man like that, a sniffy man, always make sure he has a handkerchief? Day after day, I wonder if I should offer him a handkerchief.'

'I would,' Mummy said. 'I'd buy him a whole packet.'

'I know you would,' Daddy replied. 'You don't mind confrontation. But what if this man thought I was being rude? You know, trying to make a point. Rather than just being helpful. I have to sit opposite him every day – I don't want things to be frosty.'

'Could you not just sit in a different carriage?' I asked.

Daddy looked up at me as if I'd just turned into a crested newt. 'Everyone has their seat, Chloe,' he said. 'Everyone always sits in the same seat. That way you know where you are, and where everyone else is, and nothing ever changes.'

Poor Daddy, I thought. He's not the sort of person who always sits in the same seat. He's the sort of person who invents complicated games in the garden like Canoe Wars and One-Eyed Stephen.

On Thursday Mummy had a bad day. She told us all about it while we were eating dinner. It had been raining in the morning so we'd done the school run in the car when we usually walk. Mummy doesn't like driving. Last December we were playing *Now That's What I Call Christmas CD 2* in the car and it got stuck and ever since then that's the only thing you can listen to and that's not even the one with all the good Christmas songs on so we usually don't listen to anything at all. Instead of music this morning William D was talking non-stop.

'Would you rather be called Ed, or MechaTron?' he

asked. 'Mummy, would you rather be called Ed, or MechaTron?'

'Ed,' Mummy replied as she pulled out into the traffic on Holly Street.

'Would you rather have green hair or blue feet? Mummy, would you rather have green . . .'

'Blue feet,' Mummy said impatiently as we waited at the lights. It had started raining.

'Mummy, would you rather be a brick wall, or be called Simon?'

'Oh, look, William D, you know I love you very much but please stop talking for a bit, will you?'

There's never anywhere to park when we drive to school, the whole street is full of big, black four-wheel drive cars. Imogen's mummy has the biggest and blackest one of them all and always parks it on the bus stop even though the school is forever sending letters reminding parents not to park there. So we ended up having to park on a double yellow line on Lords Road which you're not allowed to do but Mummy says isn't as naughty as parking in a bus stop. Lords Road is the next street over, so we were a bit late and a bit wet because it was still raining. Anyway, after Mummy kissed us goodbye, she had a quick chat to the other mummies.

'Do you have odd socks on, Polly?' Imogen's mummy, Ellen, asked.

Mummy looked down. One of her socks was blue, and the other was black. 'Yes, it seems I do,' she said, laughing. 'That's the problem when you get dressed in the dark.'

'Did you get your hair cut in the dark as well?' Ellen asked, then laughed loudly to show it had been a joke.

But it wasn't a joke, it was mean. It was the sort of thing Imogen might have said. Mummy said she'd wanted to storm off after that, but she couldn't because she had to chase after William D, who'd run off as usual. By the time she'd caught him and walked out of the school gates, the rain had stopped and she'd completely forgotten about the car. Mummy works part-time in an office in Weyford and it was only when she got home after work that she realised the car wasn't there outside the house. She ran back to Lords Road to find she had a parking ticket.

Then when we all got home, she found the boiler wasn't working and the plumber can't come until next week. We all had to go over to the Bellamys' for a bath which was fun but chaotic, especially when William D poured all of Vicky Bellamy's shampoo into the tub because it's the same colour as his bubble bath. We all thought it was huge fun to walk back across the road in our pyjamas as the wind blew leaves past our noses. But when we got in William D asked if he could play BattleMasters on the iPad and Mummy said, 'Of course not, it's bedtime.' And William D had a meltdown.

'I haven't played all day,' he wailed.

'You played for half an hour this morning,' Mummy

65

reminded him. 'You're obsessed with that game. I think you need help.'

'He doesn't need any help,' Daisy said. 'Yesterday he beat the boss on level six.'

After William D had gone to bed, Daisy and I came downstairs. Mummy said if we did our homework we could watch a programme before our bedtimes. In the kitchen Mummy was opening a cardboard box that had been waiting for us when we got home. She pulled out a very small turkey and rested it on the counter just as Daddy came in from work.

'That's the biggest pigeon I've ever seen,' he said. 'Did Clematis bring that in?'

'It's a turkey,' Mummy said. 'I saw on Money Saver Special that if you order turkeys online and freeze them now, you can escape the inflated prices close to Christmas.'

'The advantage of waiting until closer to Christmas, though,' Daddy said, 'is that the turkeys are bigger.'

Mummy glared at him. 'We have no money, John. I'm trying to make savings. Besides, it looked bigger on screen. Will that be enough for a family of six?'

'Yeah, just do lots of potatoes,' Daddy said. 'Anyway, I have some news.'

Daddy's News

A short play by Chloe Deal

Int: Kitchen. Night. Present are Mummy, Chloe, Daisy, Daddy and a small turkey.

Daddy: I've been head hunted.

Daisy and Chloe: Yay!

Mummy: Really? By whom?

Daddy: A company called EuroComp. They're paying lots more money, and I'd be managing a big team of programmers.

Mummy: (bending to put turkey in fridge) Where is it based?

Daddy: Eindhoven.

Mummy: (muffled) Oh, not a great commute. You'll have to drive, I suppose. The A287 can get pretty busy around Basingstoke.

Daddy: (surprised) Basingstoke? Why would I go through Basingstoke?

Mummy: (standing up) That's how you get to Andover.

Daddy: Not Andover. Eindhoven. In Germany.

Daisy and Chloe are listening to this conversation with interest, looking back and forth between Mummy and Daddy like a tennis match.

67

[Long silence.]

Mummy: You're going to commute to Germany?

Daddy: It's a lot more money.

Mummy: How much more money?

Daddy: Twice as much as I'm paid currently.

Mummy: That is a lot more money.

Daddy: Just think what we can do with it. We can get the house decorated. Get a new boiler.

Chloe: Buy a bigger turkey.

Mummy: Have you said yes?

Daddy: Not yet. I thought it best to talk to you first.

Mummy notices Daisy and Chloe are listening.

Mummy: (to Daddy) We'll talk about this later.

Weyford's Got Talent

The next day Mr Bolli told us that all the pupils who had auditioned for parts in *Aladdin* were to go to the hall in last period. But I wish he hadn't told us this in first period. We were excited about it all day and it was really hard to concentrate on the lesson, which was maths. We were learning about trajectories. I know all about trajectories because of BOOMBall but it's hard to translate what you can see and feel into diagrams and numbers. I suppose that's what maths is, a special language to describe the world. Tobias is very good at the language of maths even if he's not so good at the language of everyday life.

Imogen was pretending she wasn't bothered whether she got the part or not but I could tell she was, because she kept chewing a strand of her hair which is something she does when she's nervous. I wondered if she was wishing she'd auditioned for an alternate part in case she didn't get Jasmine. We talked about nothing else at lunchtime. Even Tobias kept pacing up and down in the playground. Finally it was time to go, and at 2.40 p.m. we all shuffled in to the hall and dragged chairs across the floor, the boys trying to make as much noise as possible.

'Quieten down, quieten down,' Madame Adams shouted over the racket. 'You're all going to have to learn to control yourselves a lot better than that if this is to be a successful performance. Mr Grover told me there needs to be a significant improvement on last year's play. We got terrible reviews from the Weyford Gazette.'

'We should never have done *Grease: the Musical*,' Mr Bolli said, shaking his head.

'Well that's easy to say in hindsight,' Madame Adams said. 'But none of us knew poor Charlie Odell was going to develop that terrible allergy to hair cream. Or that Millie Radigan was going to slide into the orchestra pit.'

'She went like-a greased lightning,' Mr Bolli said and we all laughed.

So then they told us who was going to play who or do what. Everyone looked really nervous. They did the smaller parts and stage crew first. Daisy got a non-speaking part as a palace guard. She didn't look pleased about it. Tamsin was in the lighting team, which I thought probably wasn't a good idea as it involved climbing up on scaffolding and handling heavy lights. Emily got a part as a friendly merchant which she seemed happy with. She had one line, which was 'Quick, hide in here!'

They left the bigger parts until last, which made us feel really nervous, which is why they did it. There were a few Year Sixes who didn't have speaking parts yet and none of us were sure whether the last few parts would be for us or if we'd miss out altogether. Most of the non-speaking roles had gone now. If I didn't get a speaking part, I might end up in the chorus, or just one of the townsfolk, or possibly even no part at all! As each part was read out I got more and more anxious. I glanced over at Imogen who I could tell was pretending not to be nervous but she was chewing her hair like mad.

'The part of the Caliph goes to . . . Ben Ollerenshaw,' Madame Adams cried out.

Ben's friends clapped him on the back. Ben was right for that role, I thought. The Caliph is a well-meaning but indecisive character. Ben takes ages to decide what flavour squash he's going to have with school dinners. This meant Ben wouldn't be Aladdin. Indren Patel had got the part of the Thief Leader already so it was between Thomas and Oliver.

'The part of the Monkey . . . goes to Sophie Linklater!' Mr Bolli said.

The monkey doesn't have any actual words, but lots of ooh oohs and aah aahs. Sophie seemed happy with the role. She does gymnastics and would be good at all the leaping around.

'The part of the Magic Carpet goes to . . . Tobias Roper!' Madame Adams cried.

Tobias leapt up onto his seat and raised his fists in victory. Just about everyone cheered, though I saw Imogen shaking her head.

'The part of the Genie goes to Hannah Wilson!' Mr Bolli said.

Hannah was sitting next to Imogen and Imogen clapped her on the shoulder before darting a quick look at me. I pretended I wasn't looking and inspected my fingernails instead.

'The part of the Grand Vizier, goes to . . .' Madame Adams waited, and waited. I swallowed nervously. Out of the corner of my eye I felt Imogen turn her head to look at me again.

'. . . Chloe Deal!'

I felt a mixture of relief and disappointment. I had a part. It was obviously the cackle that had won it for me and tripping over the microphone stand hadn't harmed my chances as much as I'd feared. Also, I knew it was probably the best role for me. But still a part of me had wanted to get the role of Jasmine, to beat Imogen. I looked over at her. She still looked nervous. Her place wasn't secure yet. Was it wrong of me to want her to miss out?

As Mr Bolli began speaking, Imogen grabbed a strand of hair and started chewing it again.

'The part of Jasmine, goes to . . .'

And now he REALLY drew it out. He waited, and waited, and waited, until the room was full of tension and our hair stood on end.

'. . . Imogen Downing!'

'Yay!' Nice Chloe shouted out loud.

'Boo!' Mean Chloe said in secret.

'And the final part, Aladdin himself,' Madame Adams said, 'goes to . . . and I won't hold you in suspense for long this time because the bell is about to go . . . Thomas Cartwright!'

And for the third time, I had mixed feelings as I clapped. I was pleased for Thomas, and not at all surprised he'd got the part over Oliver who is possibly the worst actor there has ever been. But this meant Thomas would be playing Jasmine's boyfriend. And I was playing the meanie who was trying to keep them apart. I knew I could play the meanie. And so that just left the keeping them apart bit. As we left the hall, I found myself walking alongside Imogen in the crush.

'Bad luck,' she said. 'But I think you'll make a good villain.'

'Well, acting is all about being something you're not,' I replied. 'I'm sure you'll make a good princess.'

'I already have some silk dresses I can wear,' she said. 'Mummy bought them for me when we went to Marrakech in spring half term. Maybe you could borrow some of your mother's old clothes? She has lots.'

I stopped and glared at her.

'I'm joking,' she said in the same sort of way her mummy did. Then she paused before continuing. 'Look, Chloe. I know we haven't always been best friends, but we're going to be rehearsing together a lot over the next few weeks. Shall we try and get on?'

I was surprised by this. And a bit suspicious. And also

73

annoyed that I hadn't been the one to try and mend the bridge. But I nodded.

'Yes, OK,' I said.

'I know it's a few weeks away,' she said. 'But we're planning a Halloween party at our house. The orangery is finished now and there's plenty of space for guests. I'll ask Mummy to send you an invitation, and Emily too because she has a part in the play. Loads of people are going to be there.'

'Thank you,' I said, automatically. But I was still suspicious as I grabbed my bag and headed for the door. Was this a trick?

Tricks

'Is it a trick?' I asked Cara, as we hummed our way down York Road the next Wednesday morning. 'Do you think Imogen is pretending to be nice?'

'She might be,' Cara said as she stopped to let a cat cross the road.

It was Simon, the Bellamys' cat. He paused and smiled at us with his eyes before carrying on. When cats look at you and close their eyes that means they're smiling at you.

'Then again, it might be genuine. People change, Chloe. At least, when they're young. Once you get to my age you sort of get stuck in your ways.'

'You're not old,' I said. Though I had no idea how old she was.

I heard a fox call out from the direction of the recreation ground at the bottom of the road. That's another reason I like to help Cara, even if it's hard to get out of bed so early. I love wildlife and you see so much more of it at this time, when there are no people about, and no noise except for the cheery hum of the float. In the summer, as the light was breaking, you could hear the dawn chorus as hundreds of birds began calling for the morning to hurry up and arrive. But it was the middle of September now. The mornings were chilly and it wouldn't get light for another hour.

Cara stopped the float and grabbed two red top milk bottles. Before she went to deliver them though, she stopped and turned to me.

'But some people only pretend to change,' she said. 'Some people put on a mask and pretend to be something they're not.'

I frowned. Was that what I was doing? It was OK if it was just acting, wasn't it?

'Don't ever be like that, Chloe,' she said. 'Always be true to yourself.'

I will, I thought to myself, as she disappeared into the bushes at the front of Mrs Simpson's house. I will always be true to myself.

William D, who is always true to himself, was up when I got back into the house and was eating his breakfast incredibly fast so he could go and watch telly in the playroom. Daddy had got up with him and was standing against the Aga with his eyes closed and his mouth open. He'd boiled the kettle but not got around to making his coffee yet. I finished it for him and handed it over.

'Thanks,' he said, suddenly opening his eyes.

'FinishedcanIgetdown?' William D said.

It's taken a lot of time, patience and BattleMaster figurines, but Mummy and Daddy have finally got him

76

to ask permission to leave the table. He used to just run off, scattering cutlery.

'Would you like some fruit?' Daddy asked him.

William D will eat fruit, but there is often a lot of negotiation that has to take place first.

'Can I eat it in front of the telly?'

'If you use a bowl.'

'What fruit have you got?' William D asked.

'Apple?' Daddy said.

William D frowned.

'Banana?' Daddy said.

William D shook his head.

'Raspberries?'

'I don't really like any of those fruits, and for that reason, I'm out.'

'This isn't *Dragon's Den*,' Daddy said. 'Have an apple.'
William D took the apple and raced off, hiccupping because he'd eaten too quickly.

I asked Daddy if he was going to take the job in Germany. I'd been thinking about this quite a lot over the last week or so, since he'd told us about the job offer. There had been a few whispered discussions between Mummy and Daddy and they'd go all quiet when I came into the room, then start talking about something really boring.

'I don't think so,' he said. 'The money would be useful, but I'd never get to see you lot. And Mummy needs me around the house. She can't do it all on her own.'

I tried not to look at the pile of washing-up in the sink that Daddy hadn't done last night after dinner. I walked up to him and gave him a hug.

'Good,' I said. 'I'm glad. I like having you around.'

Strange Day

Something strange happened at school that day. Imogen was nice to me. I was standing with Emily as usual as we were waiting to go into class. Imogen walked past and slowed down. This is usually when she says something mean that doesn't sound mean on the surface but has lots of bubbling meanness underneath. Once she said that she and her mummy had donated some cans of food to a foodbank and wasn't it a great idea and had my family ever used a foodbank? And another time she asked me if I had a boyfriend and I said 'NO!' really loudly and she said. 'No, didn't think so.'

So anyway I was on my guard as she approached.

'Hi Chloe,' she said.

'Hello Imogen,' I said.

'Are you looking forward to our Halloween Party?'

'Err, yes?' I said warily.

'Great,' she said. 'I like your braid, by the way.'

'. . . Thanks,' I said, waiting for the insult.

But that was all. She walked off. Emily and I watched her go.

'I'm looking forward to the party as well,' Emily called after her, then she looked at me, puzzled. 'What was all that about?'

Triangle (Part Two)

'Put your shoes on!' Mummy shouted at William D as he raced past her towards the TV room after finishing his breakfast on Friday. You have to start early telling William D to put his shoes on because you have to tell him at least five times before he'll actually do it. She came into the kitchen, sighed and started looking through the post which had just been delivered.

'Bills, bills, bills,' she said.

'Well, give them to Bill then,' Daddy said.

But Mummy just gave him a withering look.

Daddy grimaced and carried on with what he was doing, which was looking for a clean spoon. There were loads of dirty spoons in the sink but he hadn't got around to washing them up last night and Mummy was refusing to do it.

As I was finishing my cornflakes, Jacob came in through Front Door, back from his shift at the all-night garage. He's the best of us at opening Front Door. Mummy is the worst. She always comes in through the back door now that the side walkway has been cleared.

I watched Jacob walk down the hall, checking his phone. He's started growing a beard but it's a bit scratchy at the moment and makes him look older. He looked up and saw me glaring at him. He frowned and turned to escape.

'Don't run away,' I said. 'I want to talk to you.'

He sighed and came in to the kitchen. He got the orange juice carton out of the fridge and came to sit at the table with me.

'Go on,' he said.

'Why did you go out with Taffeta the other day? I thought you were going out with Charlie?'

He tutted. 'I'm not "going out" with Charlie. We've just gone out a few times.' I must have looked puzzled because he went on. 'I mean. She's not my girlfriend. Just because you go on a few dates with someone doesn't make them your girlfriend.'

'So is Tabitha your girlfriend?' I asked.

'No,' he said. 'Look, Tabs is going through a difficult time at the moment. I'm trying to be supportive.'

'What sort of difficult time?' I asked.

'A death in the family.'

'Oh my gosh,' I said. 'Poor Tabitha.'

'Yeah, she loved that guinea pig. Anyway, she asked if I'd go to the cinema with her. I couldn't say no, could I?'

Yes, Bad Chloe thought.

'No,' Good Chloe said.

'I had no idea Charlie was going to be here,' Jacob said. 'She wasn't supposed to find out.'

'Why would that matter if you and Tabitha are just friends?'

Jacob frowned at me again. 'I remember,' he said. 'When you only came up to my knee. I used to hold your hand all the way down to the park because you fell over a lot.'

'I still fall over a lot,' I said, rubbing my knee where I'd bruised it at school the day before.

'Now you're grilling me about relationships,' Jacob pointed out.

William D came charging back into the kitchen, wielding a huge plastic sword. He swung it and knocked a bowl of cereal off the table. It shattered all over the floor. Mummy screamed.

'I'll get it, I'll get it,' Daddy said.

'Ow!' William D said as he stood on a sharp piece of bowl.

'Did I not tell you a hundred times to put your shoes on?' Mummy asked him, lifting him up onto the counter so she could inspect his foot. 'These children!'

'They're just testing the boundaries,' Daddy said, trying to calm her down.

'How can they not know where the boundaries are? I show them EVERY DAY!' Mummy pointed out. 'I really don't think I could mark out the boundaries any more clearly. PUT YOUR SHOES ON, DAISY!'

'Emily says you're a typical man,' I said to Jacob as he bent down to wipe up the spilled cereal with some kitchen towel.

'What's one of those, then?'

'Never telling the complete truth. Always hiding their true feelings. Embezzling funds from offshore bank accounts.'

'Is Dad a typical man?' Jacob asked.

Jacob started calling Daddy Dad and Mummy Mum when he was twelve. Imogen calls her Daddy Toby and her Mummy Ellen. I'm never going to stop calling my parents Daddy and Mummy. That's who they are. We paused for a moment to watch Daddy, who had given up looking for a spoon and was now eating his cereal with the tip of William D's sword.

'No.' I shook my head. 'Daddy's not typical of anything.'

'OK,' Jacob said. 'Next time I'm in a tricky spot, relationship-wise, I'll ask myself WWDD.'

'What's that stand for?'

'What Would Dad Do?' Jacob said.

'As long as you don't ask yourself WWWDD,' I said.

He furrowed his brow. 'What's that?'

'What Would William D Do?'

He nodded and frowned at his phone.

'What's wrong?' I asked.

'I'm out of phone credit,' he said. 'I have to fire up the laptop and send stupid emails to people because I can't text. Who emails in this day and age?'

'Can't you buy more credit?' I asked.

'Not until payday,' he said. 'Already had to borrow £20 off my friend Rob.' He looked up at Daddy hopefully.

'Don't look at me,' Daddy said. 'I don't have any money either.'

'You can have some of my credit,' I told him. 'I have a £10 card I don't need.'

'I can't take your credit,' Jacob said. 'But thank you Chloe, that's really kind.'

But I ran up to my room and got the card with the credit on then ran back down and handed it to him.

'Please take it,' I said. 'You can pay me back when you get paid.'

He paused a moment before taking it. 'Thanks,' he said. 'I owe you!'

Yes you do, I thought.

Fourteen Days

It was raining again, so we drove to school. As soon as Mummy started the engine William D started talking about his birthday again. The only thing he likes better than quizzes is talking about his birthday. It's been the same since he could talk. His birthday is on the 10th of December, which Mummy says is not great timing.

It would have been better if he'd been born in the summer, like me, then he would have six months looking forward to his birthday after Christmas. As it is, there are just fourteen days of the year when he's looking forward to Christmas and not in full planning mode for his birthday. As soon as Christmas is over, he starts asking how many days till his next birthday and he's outraged when he hears how far away it is. He spends ages planning outlandish parties and thinking of amazing presents he's going to get. To keep him happy, Mummy helps him make lists. He has a present list, which gets stuck to the fridge, so he can keep adding to it during the year. It's currently quite long and includes the following:

Skylanders figures
BattleMaster figures
Pokémon figures
My Little Pony figures (not Pinkie Pie)
Wii game
PlayBox IV
MatchAttax cards
MatchAttax album
BattleMaster books
Pizza

He also has a list of people he wants to invite to his party that gets longer and longer too. It's all the children in his class, plus some of the children in other classes, then some children he used to go to nursery with, then friends and relatives, including Uncle Ryan, though Mummy said he probably wouldn't be able to come because it was so far. He also invited me and Daisy and one friend for each of us, then Mummy has added some children who aren't even in his school but whose parents Mummy is friendly with and who invited William D to their child's party.

'Who's Hattie?' William D asks, inspecting the list.

'She probably won't come,' Mummy replies. 'But I have to invite her because you went to her *Frozen* party last year.'

Sometimes people are crossed off the list if William

D has a row with them at school. William H has been scratched out and written back on four times.

Last week William D said, 'Mummy, Zach hasn't had his invitation yet.'

'Zach's not on the official approved list,' Mummy said, snatching it off the fridge. 'Look you crossed him off after he threw a conker at you.'

'But he's my BEST FRIEND,' William D cried, collapsing on the floor in floods of tears that I suspected weren't real but looked genuine. Mr Bolli would have been impressed with his performance. 'I've told him he's invited.'

'Fine, fine,' Mummy sighed. 'Give him this.' She scribbled the details of the party on a piece of paper and thrust it into William D's book bag.

He also spends a lot of time imagining the perfect party.

'I'm going to have a Skylanders party,' he'll say. 'With DragonTown characters and BattleMaster decorations and a My Little Pony entertainer, but not Pinkie Pie.'

We're not sure why he doesn't like Pinkie Pie but she's always the baddie when he plays My Little Pony. I'm too old for My Little Pony but I sometimes graciously agree to join in with William D and Daisy because I know they want me to and they need someone to organise their game.

William D changes his mind a lot about the perfect party. If he's just eaten a slice of pizza he'll want to have a pizza-making party. If we've just been for a swim at the leisure centre he'll want a pool party. In the summer he wanted a camping party.

'Your birthday's in December,' Mummy reminded him. 'By all means have a camping party, but I'm not coming.'

One present that's been on the list since last Boxing Day is a PlayBox IV, the latest games console. There have been adverts about it on the telly for ages and William D actually records them and watches them over and over while Daisy and I roll our eyes and say 'Can we watch the actual programme now?'

'Look at it,' William D says, touching the screen. 'It's so beautiful.' The other thing he does is go on YouTube and watch videos of other people playing the games. I don't get that at all. Sometimes you'll have William D watching Stampy on YouTube and Daisy watching Zoella on the laptop and I just shake my head and go off and do something more productive like arguing with my friends on AppChat.

'We have the Wii,' Mummy says to William D when he asks about the Playbox. 'We have 2016 Olympics.'

But he's not interested in those. The PlayBox IV has lots of games with swords and guns and cars crashing into each other. It's really expensive though, and Mummy told him we can't afford it. Daisy and I would quite like a PlayBox IV as well because you can get Mega Dance Jukebox Karaoke which I played at Hannah's one time and is totally awesome.

'It's OK,' William D said. 'I'll just get Santa to bring me the PlayBox for Christmas. He gets elves to build all the toys for free.'

Mummy sighed and said, 'That's up to Santa, you'll have to be very good between now and then.'

So William D got me and Daisy to help him make a mega star chart which was too big to fit on the fridge and had to go on the wall. We call it the Lost Galaxy.

'I'm going to fill this with stars before Christmas,' he said, his eyes shining. 'Then Santa will HAVE to bring me the PlayBox IV.'

'Well you're not off to a great start,' Mummy said, brandishing a note he'd brought home from school today.

To be fair though, he hasn't had a note for a while. He's been eating his school dinners lately and has even got a few stars dusting the Lost Galaxy. But he still has lots of accidents.

ST ANDREW'S INFANT SCHOOL

INCIDENT/ACCIDENT REPORT

Day: Mon, Tue, Wed, Thu, Fri

Child's Name: William D

Class: Bumblebees

Details of Incident/Accident:

William D bumped heads with another child while playing conkers. The teacher was notified and he was monitored for the rest of the day.

Signed:

Mrs Gurney

School Secretary

'They never give you enough information in these notes,' Mummy said. 'Who was the other child?'

'I don't know,' William D replied. 'But he cried and I didn't. So I won.'

'I think we need to explain the rules of conkers to you again,' Mummy said. 'Do you behave yourself at school?'

William D looked outraged that she'd even asked the question but Mummy narrowed her eyes suspiciously. The phone rang just then and she went to answer it.

'Oh, hi,' she said. 'What's up?' Mummy listened for a bit and I could see her expression changing from a frustrated one to a grumpy one to a cross one. I could only hear her side of the conversation and didn't know who she was speaking to. I sat and used my Observation skills to try and guess what was going on.

'You don't remember saying that?' Mummy said.

'. . .'

'Well I do. You said "Why not come and stay at Christmas?"'

Ah, I thought. She was talking to Daddy, who was working in London that day.

'. . .'

'Well that's not how they interpreted it, clearly,' Mummy snapped.

'. . .'

'No, they're arriving on Christmas Eve for heaven's sake. And staying until New Year's Eve.'

'. . .'

'I couldn't say no. Not after you invited them.'

'. . .'

'Well you talk to them. He's your brother.'

Ah, that cleared that up. They were talking about the Cooper-Deals. It seemed they were coming for Christmas. Yay!

'OK, fine. Your dinner is in the freezer.'

Mummy hung up, looking cross.

'Is everything OK, Mummy?' Daisy asked, looking worried.

'Yes, everything's fine,' Mummy said. 'But I think we're going to need to get another turkey. Either that or engage in some serious FHB.'

'What's FHB?' Daisy asked.

'Family Hold Back,' Mummy explained. 'It means we'll have to eat sparingly and let our guests have most of the food.'

I wasn't sure I was happy about that. I can eat LOADS at Christmas.

'So are the Cooper-Deals coming for Christmas?' Daisy asked, her eyes shining excitedly.

'Yes they are,' Mummy said pinching the bridge of her nose. 'Yes they are.'

Daddy phoned Auntie Moira when he got home but he's too nice to say no to people and he had sort of invited them to come for Christmas after all, so he had to go along

93

with it. Daisy, William D and I were delighted. We loved having people to stay. While I was brushing my teeth, I heard Mummy and Daddy talking about it downstairs and I crept to the spot I sit in when I want to listen to them.

'It's not that I don't like them,' Mummy was saying. 'It's just that we all work so hard, and we're so busy, I want Christmas to be a restful time. For just us.'

'We'll all do our bit,' Daddy said. 'Moira and Lisa can help around the place. Desmond's good with DIY and what-not. Grandpa Jim can . . . Grandpa Jim can go through the *TV Times* with a highlighter.'

'But what about the mould?' Mummy said. 'The flappy wallpaper? The squeaky floorboards, the dodgy electrics? We'll have to get them sorted before we have a tribe of your relatives descend on us.'

There was a long pause before Daddy responded. I could hear the telly. I could hear they were watching *Dinner Date*.

'Maybe I should take that job in Eindhoven,' Daddy said. 'Just for a while. Until we get the house fixed up. Then I can find something else closer to home.'

'I don't want you away all week, John,' Mummy said. 'We'll all miss you too much. And you don't want that either.'

'It won't be for ever,' Daddy said 'Look. I got us into the mess. I need to get us out of it.'

Suddenly I wished I hadn't complained about the wallpaper.

All the Leaves are Brown

The weather has turned cold. Autumn has properly arrived and there's a chilly wind. Mummy went in to see William D's teacher to ask for more feedback about him and Mrs Duvall said she'd start something called a 'behaviour diary'.

'If you get good reports from school,' Mummy told William D, 'then we can add more stars to your star chart.' William D frowned.

In other news, Daddy has accepted the job in Germany. Jacob has gone on two more dates with Tabitha and we haven't heard 'Bang Bang' by Jessie J for some time. I'm having trouble remembering my lines from *Aladdin*. I'm starting to wish I was the carpet-seller instead of Emily because she only has one line and gets to wear a brilliant hat with a tassel. Daisy is having problems too – she's not happy about being a palace guard. I'm surprised Daisy doesn't want to be on stage. She loves looking at herself in the mirror and trying on different outfits. She sings into her deodorant bottle and practises looking sad and happy and confused. She's a natural at acting. But today she told Mummy she didn't want to be in the play at all. Mummy looked pained and sat down with her to have a talk.

'I'll never ask you to do anything you don't want to do, Daisy,' she began.

'What about going to Sainsbury's?' Daisy said.

'That doesn't count, everyone has to go to Sainsbury's.'

'What about going to bed? I never want to go to bed.'

'Stop changing the subject. The thing is, I've made a series of extremely complicated arrangements involving pick-ups, drop-offs, lift-sharing and general child-care. All of my scheming relies on you being at school late on Wednesdays for your play rehearsals. If you pull out of the play, then I'll have to rearrange everyone's lives for the next three months.'

'OK, I'll do the play,' Daisy said, looking glum.

'Thank you,' Mummy said. 'I'll make it up to you.'

I felt a bit sorry for Daisy. She's always just going along with things. It's tricky being the middle child. I suppose I'm a middle child too, but we don't really count Jacob because he's so much older. After school I suggested to Daisy that we go out to the Secret Garden. We stomped through the crispy leaves, breathing in the sharp, earthy smells of autumn. Jacob had mowed the lawn to get money for phone credit so the grass was nice and short. Clematis stalked around the newly-weeded beds grumpily. He likes the garden to be overgrown to attract wildlife so he can kill it. Daisy and I made the Secret Garden underneath the rhododendron at the back, where the summerhouse was before it burned down. Jacob helped us put up a canopy made of tarpaulin and we have some old plastic chairs and a table. We decorated it with flowers in pots and Mummy got us some flashing solar lights which come on every night as it gets dark. It's not really very secret, but it just means grown-ups aren't allowed. We sat at the table. We had something important to talk about.

We shivered as we sat and looked at the script together. I asked her why she didn't want to be a palace guard. It turns out there's one scene in which the palace guards have to troop up to the edge of the stage and salute.

'Are you really worried about that?' I asked.

'Worried as a rain coat,' she said. 'It's too much. All those people watching me.'

'They're not watching you,' I said. 'They're watching a palace guard from hundreds of years ago. As soon as the curtain goes up, they'll be transported back to a time of pharaohs and viziers, princesses and magic.' I think Mr Bolli's enthusiasm for the theatre was starting to rub off on me.

Daisy eyed me doubtfully.

'My sword is made from Bacofoil,' she said. 'I don't think that's going to transport anyone.'

PART THREE
October

Behaviour Diary — William D   Oct 3

William D received a bump on the
head and got wet when he
pulled the turtle tank over
during horseplay.
One of the turtles is still missing.
When we asked him how it happened
he said he had LOST HIS MEMORY.

He is now under a BLACK CLOUD.

S. Duvall.

Voices

Today at school all the Year Sixes had a rehearsal for the play. We've been practising our lines in English class but this was the first time we'd gone into the hall to practise. Mr Bolli gave us all a talking-to before we started.

'Think about your position on stage. Think about *enunciating* your words.' As he spoke, Imogen sidled up beside him and started nodding along, as if she was Mr Bolli's assistant or something. She is so annoying.

'You can read from the script, and we're not doing any of the songs,' Mr Bolli went on. 'So we should-a be able to get through this before the bell goes. OK?'

'OK,' some of us mumbled.

'OK?!' Mr Bolli repeated.

'OK!' we chorused.

'And guys,' Imogen added, clapping her hands together. 'Let's all have fun today.'

'Err, yes. Thanks Imogen,' Mr Bolli said.

'Great *enunciating*,' Bad Chloe said to Imogen as we made our way up on to stage.

'Thanks,' she said. She just doesn't get sarcasm.

The rehearsal didn't include the whole cast, just the lead actors, but even so, the stage was pretty full. We got through it OK and most people remembered where they were supposed to stand and what they were supposed to say.

Mr Bolli caught up with me as we were leaving. 'Chloe, can I have the word?'

'OK, Mr Bolli,' I said.

'When you talk on stage. You sometimes sound a bit . . . I don't-a mean to be rude, but like-a wood. Yes?'

'Wooden?' I asked.

'Yes. Well maybe not wooden, but you read everything in the same voice. With an American accent. You know how on *X Factor*, Simon Cowell is saying "Make this song your own. Use your own voice."'

'Yes,' I said. I was on familiar ground with *The X Factor*.

'You're using a different voice. Not your own voice.'

'But I'm acting.'

'Why you need an acting voice? You have a lovely voice of your own. Use that.'

'But what about when I'm the Vizier? Shouldn't I use the Vizier's voice?'

'No. Just use your own voice,' Mr Bolli said. 'Always use your own voice.'

Eindhoven

We all really missed Daddy that week – the first week he worked in Germany. He'd often come home late before, but we usually saw him at least once a day during the week. Now we knew he wouldn't be around until Saturday morning, it was really sad. Mummy found it difficult too, I think, though she was really cheerful all the time and I think was making a special effort. She cooked lots of yummy meals and bought us some new DVDs and made popcorn.

But all week our house felt like it had a hole in it.

Private Daisy

On Wednesday morning as we were getting ready for school, William D ran off upstairs and came back carrying a can of hair mousse which he handed to Daisy. Lately he's been asking Daisy to help him style his hair in the mornings. 'Not like 1D, not like 1D,' he shouts. 'Like the other one.' We're not really sure which 'other one' he means, but Daisy knows how he likes it.

So Daisy squirted a handful of mousse onto her palm and expertly styled William D's hair while he nodded approvingly. I rolled my eyes. I don't get why people spend so much time over grooming. I looked at myself in the mirror. Actually, my hair was a bit messy. And I still had some breakfast on my chin. Maybe it wouldn't hurt to have a bit of a tidy.

So when Mummy came thundering back down the stairs, she found us all jostling for position in front of the mirror, brushing, styling, wiping, pouting. Daisy went to adjust William D's hair one more time but he held up a hand to stop her.

'It's perfect,' he said.

'Oh, sweet,' Mummy said, and ran off to grab the

camera but she was too late because we'd all finished and had run off by the time she came back. As we left the house a huge gust of wind whipped up a fine spray of water droplets from the trees on York Road. Golden leaves whirled around us and Mummy whooped as her skirt flew up.

William D clutched his hair. 'My do!' he cried. 'My do!'

After school was the first full rehearsal, with the whole cast. It mostly went pretty well. Imogen and Thomas both knew almost all of their lines. I got a lot of mine right but had to read the script a few times. We didn't get through the whole thing because it took for ever to change the scenes because everyone had to get off first, then the next crowd of townsfolk, or thieves, or soldiers would have to squeeze on.

It's always like this in our plays. They have to make sure everyone in the whole school gets on to the stage at some point so they always have loads and loads of extras just wandering about, filling up the stage and getting in the way. It was like Waterloo Station sometimes, with people rushing back and forth not knowing where they were supposed to be.

'This needs to all-a happen a lot quicker,' Mr Bolli shouted at us. 'You need-a to move like the Ferrari, not like the London bus.'

On the other side of the stage I could see Daisy standing, waiting to come on along with the other palace guards. She was carrying her Bacofoil sword and looked really nervous. This was the scene in which she and the other guards were supposed to rush on and arrest Aladdin and drag him away.

Mr Bolli was calling out the stage directions. 'Now the townsfolk exit stage left and then the guards rush in from stage right.' Daisy must have heard this because, without waiting, she rushed on to the stage waving her sword. The other soldiers followed her.

'Too early, too early!' Mr Bolli shouted. 'Wait for the . . .'

But it was too late. The townsfolk were still clearing the stage when a dozen soldiers rushed on from the other side. In the middle, right at the front of the stage, stood Thomas and Imogen. Daisy skidded to a stop just before she reached Thomas but the other soldiers kept coming out, one after the other. There wasn't room for everyone and Daisy found herself pushed across the stage, into Thomas. She grabbed hold of him and they fell right off the front of the stage with a great crash.

'Thomas!' Imogen cried.

'Sorry!' Daisy said.

I jumped down to help Thomas. 'Are you all right?' I said, grabbing his hand and helping him up.

Mr Bolli rushed over to check he was OK.

'I think so,' he replied. 'The stage isn't very high.'

'It's because children always fall off stages,' Mr Bolli explained.

'Thanks,' Thomas said, smiling at me.

I grinned back, then realised I was still holding his hand. I let it go as Imogen swept up and took Thomas's arm.

'Are you hurt?' she asked dramatically. 'Can you go on?'

I watched as she swooned all over him and sniffed. She is so fake.

Once we were sure Thomas was OK, Mr Bolli made us all stand up on the stage and gave us another good talking-to about following stage directions. 'You cannot let this sort of thing happen on the night,' he said, waving his arms dramatically.

'It wasn't our fault,' Sophie said.

'Yes, it was Daisy Deal's fault,' Imogen said.

I gave her a look but she ignored me.

'It's not one person's fault,' Mr Bolli said. 'All of you need to know where to be. All of you need to get there more quickly, without crashing into other people. You must be ready for anything.' He sighed and went on. 'You must learn to adapt yourself to the surprise or the thing that goes wrong.' He stopped and looked at us each in turn. 'Because things go wrong all the time.'

I nodded. He certainly had that right.

On the walk home, Daisy looked awful.

'Are you OK? You look sad.' I asked.

'I am. Sad as a signpost,' she agreed. 'I don't want to be a palace guard.'

'Why?' I asked. 'Just because of one little disaster? That wasn't even your fault anyway. Not entirely.'

'I ruined the whole thing,' Daisy said, downcast. 'I nearly killed your boyfriend.'

'He's NOT my boyfriend!'

'He likes you,' she said as we walked past the chip shop. I looked in but Charlie wasn't working just then.

'No he doesn't,' I replied. 'He likes Jasmine, I mean Imogen.'

'That's just in the play. You can tell he likes you because of the way he looks at you when you're not looking back at him.'

'How does he look at me?'

'Like Tash looks at Jacob.'

'WHAT? No he doesn't,' I shrieked. But inside my tummy went a bit funny.

'Anyway,' she said as we turned onto York Road. 'I just don't have what it takes to be a palace guard.'

'Well what do you want to be?' I asked.

'I don't want to be on stage at all,' she said. 'Can't I work on the sets? Or on the lights like Tamsin? There must be something else I can do that doesn't involve me being on stage.'

'Let's ask Mr Bolli about it tomorrow,' I said. I thought it was time to change the subject. I know Daisy could be brilliant if she put her mind to it. But it was obvious she wasn't in the mood to listen to me.

Shouty Dad was standing on the pavement as we walked down York Road. Shouty Dad lives opposite us and is always shouting at his children, which is why everyone calls him Shouty Dad. But today he wasn't shouting at his children, he was shouting at his car.

'WHY WON'T YOU START?!' he shouted. 'WHY WON'T YOU START?!'

We crossed over to the other side of the street to avoid him.

As soon as we got in though the back door (because Front Door was stuck again) my phone buzzed in my pocket and I went behind the sofa in the sitting room to answer it. Mummy has given me her old phone. Since the summer fair at school she's been using her new iPhone that I bid slightly too much for at the silent auction. I'm not allowed to use my phone at school, just on the walk there and back. But sometimes in the evenings and weekends Mummy lets me use it to chat with my friends. We use AppChat and it took me ages to get my head around it because people keep starting new chats instead of just using the same one and there are too many conversations going on all at once and EVERYONE gets tagged in on everything you say and everyone gets the wrong end of the stick and someone always gets cross so most of our conversations are just long, confusing arguments about who said what first about who and who started the new chat anyway and people keep leaving the group in a huff and then coming back ten minutes later when they get bored.

It's really fun!

After about fifteen minutes Daisy came and found me behind the sofa. She had changed into her favourite stripy tights and was looking more like herself but still a bit sad.

'Do you want to come and play in the Secret Garden?' she asked.

'In a bit,' I said as I texted.

But then Sophie sent a vine of a cat falling into a pond and that set everyone off sending their favourite vines of cats falling into things or off things and by the time I'd finished it was dark and Daisy was busy watching *Operation Ouch* with William D.

Sex Talk

Daddy has been working in Germany for two weeks now. I miss him so much when he's away. He tries to Skype but he's not very good at getting it to work. And our computer is a bit rubbish anyway so he mostly just phones and usually after we've gone to bed, because he's working long hours. He gets up very early on Monday mornings and takes the train to Woking, then changes for the coach to the airport. Then he gets on a plane and flies to Eindhoven where the company he's working for pick him up in a taxi. He stays in a little hotel near the office during the week and is allowed to leave early on Friday so he's able to get home before we go to bed. But the airline is one of those cheap ones that's always late, and when he gets to the airport in England he has to wait for a coach and the trains are delayed so for the last three weeks he hasn't been getting back until very late. Then he sleeps until the middle of the morning because he's so tired.

'It won't be for ever,' Mummy told me and Daisy over breakfast on Saturday. Yesterday, Daddy was so busy at his German office that he'd had to stay another night and wasn't due back until later this morning. Mummy had had no one to look after William D so she'd had to take him along with her to the school for the Sex Talk.

'You took him to the Sex Talk?' Daisy asked, eyes wide.

'What else could I do?' Mummy said. 'I gave him my iPod and clapped earphones over his ears to distract him.'

'How did the talk go?' I asked.

Daisy giggled, then I giggled. Mummy sighed.

'Well, we all sat there, and they told us about the DVD we were going to see, and then we watched the DVD. And then we were all a bit stunned, really. And then Mrs Keyne asked if anyone had any questions and only one person put up a hand,' Mummy said.

'Who?'

'William D,' Mummy said, shaking her head.

'I thought he was looking at your iPod,' Daisy said.

'So did I!' Mummy said. 'He must have decided the DVD was more interesting.'

'What was his question?'

'I didn't let him ask it,' Mummy said. 'I yanked his hand down before Mrs Keyne saw. I asked him about it on the way home but thankfully he said he couldn't remember.'

After breakfast Daisy helped me rehearse my lines. We

went upstairs to her room because it's bigger and doesn't have as much mess on the floor as mine does. We did the scene where Aladdin meets Jasmine. The Vizier only has one line, as he's hiding in a big pot spying on Aladdin, so I was doing Aladdin's lines too. Daisy was being Jasmine. She'd gone a bit overboard and was wearing a tiara and had wrapped herself in one of Mummy's scarves.

'We're only rehearsing,' I said. 'You don't need to get dressed up.'

'I'm getting into the role,' Daisy said. 'If I dress up like Jasmine, it's easier to pretend I'm her and not just myself.'

'OK,' I said. I understood.

'Oh Aladdin, my love, we must not be seen together,' Daisy said, reading from the script. 'If my father hears of our meeting, he will lock you up in the deepest dungeon.' She looked up at me and fluttered her eyelashes.

'No dungeon could ever keep me away from you,' I said. 'Now sweet Jasmine, look into my eyes and . . .' I paused, staring at the script.

'. . . and what?' Daisy asked.

'It says here . . .' I began. 'There's a . . .' But I couldn't bring myself to finish the sentence. Daisy looked down at the text.

'It says Aladdin kisses Jasmine,' she said. 'Don't worry, we can just hug. Or shake hands?'

'It's not that,' I said. 'Thomas is playing Aladdin in the play, and Imogen is Jasmine.'

'So?'

'So? So this means Thomas is going to kiss Imogen!'

Canoodling

Daddy arrived back eventually, looking exhausted. Even though I knew Mummy was cross, she still gave him a big cuddle and she cooked him bacon and eggs. Then he opened his case and gave us all presents. Daisy got a little make-up case, I got a brilliant book about drawing animals, William D got a new BattleMaster figure.

'What about Jacob?' I asked.

'I thought he'd probably just want phone credit,' Daddy said. Then he handed a parcel to Mummy, all wrapped in brown paper. She ripped it open to reveal a handbag.

'Oh my goodness,' she said. 'A Mulberry! John, we can't afford this.'

'There's no point me taking a well-paying job if we don't treat ourselves,' Daddy said.

'Thank you,' she said. 'It's beautiful. But you mustn't spend any more on me. The house needs to come first. OK?'

'OK,' he said, and they had a cuddle.

I was delighted with my book, but I sort of agreed with Mummy. I understood that Daddy needed to work in Germany to pay for the house to be fixed up, but I didn't want him to be away from us just so we could have expensive presents. We sat in the kitchen while he ate breakfast and we told him about our play.

'There's canoodling,' Daisy said, giggling.

Daddy raised his eyebrows and I explained about the kiss.

'Do you have to kiss someone?' he asked.

'NO!' I said.

'So what's the problem?' he asked.

'She doesn't want Thomas to kiss Imogen,' Daisy said. 'Thomas is her boyfriend.'

'NO HE ISN'T,' I roared.

'The thing about acting,' Daddy said, 'is that you have to be someone else when you're on stage. It won't be Thomas kissing Imogen. It'll be Aladdin kissing Jasmine.'

'Have you ever been in a play, Daddy?' I asked.

'I was in the Theatrical Society at University. I had an onstage kiss with Samantha Van Holst.' Daddy smiled and looked up at the ceiling as he remembered.

Daisy squealed and hid her face in her hands.

'I'm sure I've told you this before,' he said.

'No,' I replied. 'Tell us more about your onstage kiss.'

'Yes,' Mummy said, coming in to the kitchen. 'Tell us more about your onstage kiss, John.'

'Well, it was just a peck really. The important thing is that it's not real. It's just acting.' He stood and grabbed

Mummy, who squealed and tried to escape as he planted kisses all over her face.

I hated it when Daddy was away, but it made everything even better when he came home.

That day was a little warmer, so we spent it mostly in the garden. Daisy and I helped Daddy deadhead the straggly plants and try to get rid of some weeds. It was difficult because they were so overgrown. Clematis liked it when we weeded. He'd crouch in the bushes and leap out from time to time and pounce on Daddy's gardening gloves, scratching and biting. Daddy would shout in surprise and shake him off. I took some photos of him on my phone. I now have ninety-six photos in the CATS! folder in my photo library. 'Are they all worth keeping?' Mummy asked me when I showed her recently. 'Yes,' I told her, though some of them are quite blurry.

We watched Daddy for a while as he ripped plants up by the roots and threw them into a big yellow garden bag. I Observed a little ladybird sitting on his shoulder, watching as well.

'How can you tell which are the plants and which are the weeds?' I asked him.

'The weeds are the ones that are growing well,' he replied. 'If it's small and straggly and nearly dead then it's a plant. If it's strong and vigorous and spreading everywhere, then it's a weed.'

117

'Got it,' I said. 'What's it like, your job in Germany?'

'Everything's very modern,' Daddy said. 'Fancy offices in a huge building, bean bags and ping pong tables. We all have scooters so we can get from one end of the building to the other. Also, you have to use your computers for everything. No spreadsheets printed off. It's a totally paperless office.'

'No paper at all?'

'On my first day I tried to take in a copy of the *Guardian* – Security snatched it off me.'

'Any sniffy men?'

'No sniffy men,' Daddy said. 'Everyone has handkerchiefs in Germany. Amazing place.'

'It sounds wonderful,' I said. 'I bet you want to stay and work there for ever.'

'We'll see,' Daddy said. 'We'll see.'

When we'd finished, there wasn't much left in the flower beds.

'What we need to do is put some bushes and things in here,' Daddy said. 'Plants that will look after themselves and spread out so the weeds can't come back. I think a trip to Home 'n Garden Megastore might be in order.'

'Can I have another tester pot?' asked Daisy.

'How about a big pot of lilac paint?' replied Daddy, smiling. 'To finish your room once and for all?'

When we got home, the car full of bedding plants and paint tins, we saw someone standing on the porch.

Someone with a great shock of messy hair. It was Tabitha. We took her inside with us. Mummy appeared from the kitchen amidst the mad scramble as we all took off our coats and shoes and dropped them on the floor.

'Hello Tabitha,' she said. 'I'm not used to seeing you during daylight hours – I thought you teenagers were nocturnal!'

It was supposed to be a joke, but Tabitha looked at Mummy as though she was really insulted. Daddy escaped out into the garden, carrying some plants.

'We're going to a gig? In London?' Tabitha said, as though Mummy should have known this.

'Right you are,' Mummy said. Then she yelled upstairs. 'Jacob? Taff . . . Tabitha's here. Why don't you wait in here?' Mummy said, guiding Tabitha into the sitting room.

'I'm just coming,' Jacob shouted down.

Taffeta sighed and flopped down on an armchair. William D sat on the armrest and inquired if she might be interested in a quick game of BattleMaster. I went to sit down but Daisy pulled on my sleeve and took me out into the hall. Mummy passed on her way into the kitchen.

'Look after Tabitha,' she mouthed at us.

I nodded, but Daisy had something she wanted to say first.

'Remember Jacob stopped seeing Charlie because she smelled of vinegar?'

119

'I'm not sure that's the reason,' I said.

'I mean before,' Daisy went on impatiently. 'He doesn't like girls who smell of vinegar.'

'Right,' I said. 'OK.'

'So what if we make Taffeta smell of vinegar?' Daisy said.

'Daisy,' I said. 'You are SO clever.'

'Clever as a teacup,' she agreed.

We rushed into the kitchen.

'I thought you were looking after Taffeta,' Mummy said without looking up from her phone as she texted someone.

'Just getting her a drink,' I said. I filled a glass with tap water as Daisy rummaged around in the larder, looking for the vinegar.

'Got it!' she squeaked

'Got what?' Mummy asked, still not looking up.

'My hairband,' Daisy said.

I gave her a look, but she just shrugged.

'OK,' Mummy said.

Sometimes mobile phones are really handy for sneaking things past grown-ups. They're too busy staring at their screens to notice you carrying, say, the duvet into the garden, or a bucket of water into the house. That's how William D managed to bring that pile of leaves up to his bedroom. We stopped in the hall to discuss our tactics. Daisy suggested pouring some vinegar into the glass of water.

120

'That way it'll be on her lips so he won't canoodle with her,' she explained.

'She's not going to drink vinegar water,' I pointed out. 'We have to accidentally spill it on her.'

'How are we going to explain that?' Daisy asked. 'Oh sorry, I just spilled some of this vinegar on you that I just happened to be carrying through the sitting room.'

She was right. I put on my thinking face. Twelve seconds later, I had the answer.

'Go up to your room, and get a handkerchief,' I said.

Daisy nodded and thundered up the stairs. She was back in a flash and I took the handkerchief she gave me. I poured vinegar onto it and squeezed it tight, the sharp smell making my eyes water. We went back into the sitting room to find William D was explaining to Taffeta the differences between Earth-type Beests and Air-type Beests. She was also looking at her phone while he explained this.

'Can I play on your phone?' he asked.

'No,' she said.

'Here's some water,' Daisy said, plopping the glass of water down next to her.

Taffeta turned to look at her and as she did I dropped the handkerchief into Taffeta's handbag. Daisy and I sat opposite and smiled at her. Daisy couldn't help staring at the handbag. I could sense she was about to get the giggles. Taffeta looked up at us slightly suspiciously.

'I like your handbag,' Daisy said, stifling a chuckle.

I elbowed her and smiled even harder.

'Thank you,' Taffeta said. Then, clearly thinking she needed to make an effort with us, she said, 'How is school going?'

'Good,' Daisy said, her shoulders starting to shake.

'Good,' I said.

'Do you have a job yet?' Daisy asked.

I kicked her.

'No,' Taffeta replied. 'I'm concentrating on my studies at the moment.'

Charlie has a job, I thought. Even when she's studying. Taffeta just floated about looking pretty. It wasn't fair.

'Of course Air-type Beests have their uses,' William D went on. 'When you're in the Air, for example.'

'Oh God,' Taffeta said.

Luckily Jacob came down just then and suddenly Taffeta was all smiles again. She stood as Jacob kissed her on the cheek.

'Bye, you guys,' Jacob said to us. 'Be good for Mummy.'

'Bye, have a nice time,' Daisy said, hardly able to get the words out through the giggling. Jacob led Taffeta to Front Door.

'Wait,' I said, pointing. 'Don't forget your bag.'

Daisy was just about rolling on the floor at this point.

Taffeta turned. 'That's not my bag,' she said. She

picked up another brown bag from near the door. 'This one's mine.'

Then they were gone. Daisy stopped laughing and gave me a look of horror. I snatched the smelly old handkerchief out of Mummy's brand-new Mulberry handbag.

William D has been telling some of
the other pupils about 'the birds and
the bees.'
We had a talk to him about this
and after I discussed this with him
it seems he knows a surprising
amount.
Perhaps he picked this up from
his sisters? It's nothing to be
worried about really and he
certainly seems to have the basics
covered.

                                    S. Duvall.

Ghost Story

'Put your shoes on, Daisy,' Mummy said.

It was the last Saturday in October and we were getting ready to go to Imogen's house for the Halloween party. I felt a bit nervous but I was pleased with my dressing-up efforts. Like Mummy, I was going as a witch. I had a pointy hat made of crepe paper and a black dress with purple trim. Mummy had painted her face green and offered to do mine, but I said no. I didn't tell her it was because Thomas might be there. I did stick a wart to my cheek though. I could always take it off if Thomas was there. Daisy was dressed as Poppet, a pink Moshi Monster, but she hadn't quite got around to putting her shoes on yet. William D didn't want to go. Neither did Daddy. He'd had a big disaster at work that week and kept having to take phone calls. Mummy had insisted they come with us though.

'You don't even like Imogen's mummy,' William said to Mummy as she was trying to get him to put his coat on. Underneath he wore a skeleton costume, or skellington as he called it. 'You said she's always rude to you.'

Mummy stopped and frowned.

'You mustn't say that in front of Imogen's mummy,' she said. 'Or anyone outside our family, OK?'

'OK, Mummy,' William D said. 'What about William P? Can I tell him?'

'Is William P in our family?'

'No, but . . .'

'So no. You can't tell him. Family Deal?'

'OK,' William D said grumpily. 'Family Deal.'

'Ellen is fine,' Mummy went on. 'She sometimes says things that seem a little rude, but she doesn't mean to offend.'

'You said she was artificial,' Daisy added unhelpfully.

'I don't remember saying that,' Mummy replied. 'Put your shoes on.'

'You did,' Daisy went on. 'You said Ellen was 60% plastic and 40% make-up.'

'Well if I did say that, that was wrong of me,' Mummy said. 'Though quite funny. Now listen up all of you. The Downings have kindly invited us to their party, so I want everyone to be on their best behaviour.'

'Yes Mummy,' we all said.

'John?'

'I'll take another look at the spreadsheet . . .' Daddy was saying on the phone.

'JOHN!'

'. . . what?'

'Will you be on your best behaviour tonight?'

'Yes,' Daddy said. He looked tired to me. Poor Daddy.

'Daisy!' Mummy snapped.

'What?'

'PUT YOUR SHOES ON!'

As we left the house we saw the Shouty Dad family leaving their house too, all dressed up in Halloween gear. There was Shouty Dad, his quiet wife and the two youngest children. The oldest girl was nowhere to be seen.

'HURRY UP!' Shouty Dad shouted back towards the house. 'ALL THE SWEETS WILL BE GONE!'

We scurried past, off up York Road and right onto Middle Street towards the Downings' house. It was crispy cold and I could smell the wet leaves piled up in the gutters and somewhere someone had a bonfire going. Weyford is beautiful in the autumn – the trees are a hundred different colours and it seems everyone's wearing a lovely new coat.

'We're heading towards the posh end of town,' Daddy said as we crossed the train tracks.

It was true really. The houses on the south side of Weyford are much bigger and have huge gardens, even bigger than ours. They're not stuck to the side of another house like ours is. As we passed the row of shops near the station, we ran ahead and leapt into the chip shop to surprise Charlie.

'Agh!' Charlie screamed, pretending to be terrified, as a witch, a skellington and a Poppet leapt into the shop.

The skellington roared at her, scaring Mrs Windsor who was waiting for her small cod and chips order.

'Don't eat me,' Charlie cried. 'Here take these offerings!' She dropped some boiled sweets into our pumpkin buckets. 'And this is for Jacob,' she added, dropping a sachet of vinegar in my bucket.

I like the chip shop. It's always warm and welcoming. I like the hot smell of chips and the sharp scent of the vinegar cutting through.

'Hi Charlie,' Mummy said as she came into the shop behind us.

I could see Daddy outside on his phone, shaking his head as he tried to explain something to the person he was talking to.

'Hello Polly,' Charlie said. I like that Charlie called Mummy by her real name. 'Nice witch's outfit.'

'Thanks,' Mummy replied 'Nice, err . . . T-shirt. I would have thought you'd be at some Halloween party tonight.'

'I need to work,' Charlie said. 'I need the money for my trip.'

'What trip?' Mummy asked as Mr Vilic called through an order from the kitchen.

Charlie grabbed a battered fish with her tongs and started wrapping it for Mrs Windsor.

'Kenya,' she said. 'I'm volunteering in a school. Teaching English, helping street kids to get an education. I'll be back for Christmas.'

My heart sank and Daisy and I exchanged a look. Charlie couldn't go away – we needed to get her back together with Jacob! How could we do that if she was going off to Kenya in a few weeks? Admittedly, it did sound like she was doing some quite important work there, but this was a critical time for Charcob.

We had to go then, as a train had just come in and there was a rush of people. Charlie winked at me as we left and promised to pop around to say goodbye. Daddy was still on the phone as we came out and he trundled along behind us, still talking, telling someone to refer to the spreadsheet.

'We need to do something,' Daisy said as we set off again. 'Or else Charcob will be history. For ever.'

It was then that a plan started to form in my head. Not a Big Plan, like building Mummy's Retreat. And not a Stupid Plan, like the zip wire I strung up between Daisy's window and the apple tree. (It was lucky Mummy put a stop to that after she saw Tamsin wearing a cycling helmet and running up the stairs to have a go on it.) No, this was a very rare thing. It was a Perfect Plan. I told it to Daisy and her eyes lit up with how brilliant it was. She clapped her hands and squeaked.

'It's perfect,' she said. 'Perfect as a cake tin.'

Imogen's house is HUGE. It took us ages just to walk down the drive. There were dozens of pumpkins, all with perfectly terrifying faces glowing evilly as the candles

129

inside flickered in the thin breeze. William D walked very close to Mummy, holding her hand. Ellen answered the door. She was wearing a cat suit and looked very thin. Daddy finished his phone call.

'Ooh, how scary,' she said. 'Keep that dress away from the candle there, Polly. That looks like polyester.'

'It's a blend,' Mummy said.

Ellen brought us all in and Imogen came running up.

'Hi Chloe,' she said. 'Can I take your coat?'

'Err, OK,' I said suspiciously.

I glanced at Mummy and she raised an eyebrow. William D saw William P from school and they ran off together to terrorise people. The doorbell went again and Ellen excused herself, telling us to make ourselves at home. Imogen and her little brother Casper took us on a tour of the house and the gardens. It took for ever.

'Look how neat the garden is,' Mummy said, glaring at Daddy.

There was something odd about the garden, apart from how big it was, and the fact it had a tennis court. And a yurt. It took me a while, but then I realised what it was.

'There are no leaves on the lawn,' I said. 'Our lawn is nothing *but* leaves.'

'Oh, Mike takes care of the leaves,' Imogen said.

'Is he your gardener?' Mummy asked.

'No, he's just the leaf man,' Imogen said. 'The other gardeners do everything else.'

'How many gardeners do you have?' Mummy asked.

'Four, sometimes five,' Imogen replied airily.

'What's that over there?' Daddy said pointing to a wooden building half-hidden by the trees.

'That's Toby's sweat lodge,' Casper said. Toby is Imogen and Casper's daddy.

'Of course it is,' Daddy replied. 'What else would it be?'

'What's a sweat lodge?' I asked.

'He says it's good for cleansing his pores,' Imogen explained.

Then Imogen showed us the new extension they'd had done. She called it an orangery but it looked like a big conservatory with glass doors and skylights. There was a big table with drinks and food and a couple of dozen grown-ups talking loudly. Small children raced around, screaming. Mummy inspected the walls.

'This is amazing. John, isn't this wonderful? Oh, I want one of these.'

'You want an orangery?' Daddy asked. 'You're allergic to citrus.'

'It's not the name of the building, so much,' Mummy replied sweetly, 'as the way the wallpaper is actually glued to the wall and doesn't try to strangle you when you go to the loo at night.'

Emily appeared with Vicky. I gave her a hug. Emily's not very huggy, but she knows I am and sort of puts up with it.

Toby saw us and came over to say hello. He's quite handsome and smelled strongly of aftershave. I peered closely at him to see if his pores were cleansed. Daddy says Imogen's daddy is a 'smooth operator' and has a soft spot for Mummy and when we see him he does always seem to talk to Mummy while ignoring Daddy and anyone else who might be around.

'Hello Polly,' Toby said, smoothly. 'You're looking very glamorous. Do you have a drink?'

Daddy rolled his eyes as Mummy held out her glass. But the situation was saved by Ellen as she reappeared in her tight outfit.

'I see you've had some work done,' Daddy said.

So then Ellen started showing off about how much the orangery had cost. A small crowd of grown-ups gathered around to listen and I could see Mummy starting to look cross. Daisy had drifted off to find some of her friends. Imogen tugged my sleeve and we went off with Emily to find the other big children.

Imogen had a little summerhouse at the end of the garden, surrounded by maple trees. There was a heater in there, an electric light which looked like a gas lamp and some bean bags. When we arrived I saw Hannah and Sophie and Amelia and Oliver and Thomas who were drinking Coke and laughing. There was an empty bean bag next to Thomas and I moved towards it but Imogen got there first. In the end Emily and I squashed together on a wobbly wooden chair.

'So I was just saying to the others that it might be good if we all got together here once a week to practise our lines,' Imogen said. 'Just those of us with major parts.'

'What about Tobias?' I said. 'He's the Magic Carpet.'

Imogen laughed. 'The magic carpet is not a big part,' she said. 'He only has three lines.'

'Emily only has one,' I pointed out. 'And Oliver is just a palace guard.'

'I'm your understudy,' Oliver said, hurt.

This was true, I had to admit. The main parts all had understudies. Actors who knew all your lines and who could play your part if you were ill. Oliver was the understudy for the Vizier, but I don't think he was taking it very seriously. He admitted he hadn't actually bothered to read the script yet.

'Look, we have to work,' Imogen said. 'Tobias sometimes gets a bit . . . carried away.'

I frowned. I didn't like the way Imogen was with Tobias. He could be difficult sometimes but that just meant we needed to include him more, not less. The other thing that annoyed me about Imogen was that as we all talked I kept noticing how whenever Thomas said anything even a tiny bit funny, Imogen would laugh and laugh. I could feel my face going pink, just like Mummy's does when she's gradually getting crosser.

After a while, Oliver suggested we tell ghost stories, since it was Halloween. He reached across and turned down the lamp until it was almost completely dark. We were a long way from the house and all we could hear was the wind outside in the maple trees. It was quite spooky and I saw Imogen shuffle closer to Thomas. I think my ear lobes went white with anger. I get this trait from Mummy.

'There was this teenage boy and his girlfriend,' Oliver began. 'And they went for a drive in their car. But they ran out of petrol in the middle of nowhere.'

Everyone was totally silent as we listened to Oliver tell the story. Even the wind died down, as if it wanted to hear what would happen to the foolish teenagers.

'"I'm going to walk back to that gas station and get some petrol," the boy said. "While I'm gone, don't get out of the car, whatever you do. There's a hospital for the criminally insane near here. And last week Crazy Jimmy escaped."' Oliver's eyes widened as he paused. He was good at telling stories.

I saw Imogen lean across in the gloom so she was nearly on Thomas's bean bag.

'"Who's Crazy Jimmy?" the girl asked, eyes wide with fear. The boyfriend replied, "A madman who cuts people's heads off. Just stay in the car, whatever happens." So off goes the boyfriend, carrying an empty can of petrol. And the girl listens to some music, then she drops off to sleep as it starts to get dark.' Oliver stopped again as the wind picked up outside, a patter of rain hit the window and we all shivered. Oliver waited, and waited, and waited . . .

'BANG!' he shouted suddenly and we all screeched and leapt a mile.

Emily slipped off the wobbly chair and I had to grab her. We giggled and Imogen shushed us so Oliver could carry on.

'Suddenly there was a thud on the roof of the car,' he said. 'Then another. THUD, THUD, THUD! But the girl remembered what her boyfriend had said. "Don't get out of the car, whatever you do." So she checked all the doors were locked, turned up the music and covered her ears . . . THUD, THUD, THUD!' Oliver paused again, he had us in the palm of his hand, like Madame Adams when she was announcing the parts.

'Seven hours she was there. Seven HOURS. The car battery ran out after a while and she had to sit there, whimpering, crying and listening to the THUD of something on the roof. THUD, THUD!'

'Seven hours!' Imogen said. She rested a hand on Thomas's arm as she leaned closer.

My lips went tight, just like Mummy's do when she's really cross.

'Eventually, the police arrived and the thudding noise stopped,' Oliver went on. 'They got her out. "Run for the police car, get in, and don't look back,"' the policeman said. "Whatever you do, don't look back." So she ran for the police car and dived into the back seat, sobbing with fear. But she couldn't help herself. She had to turn around, she had to look back, to see what had been on the roof of the car . . .'

Oliver paused, Oliver waited. The wind moaned outside, the rain tickled the window pane. Oliver waited for complete quiet.

'And there, on top of the car she'd been in, she saw . . .'

But just at that moment Oliver was interrupted by a huge THUD! on the roof of the shed.

Everyone screamed. Imogen leapt into Thomas's arms and there was a mad scramble as everyone else panicked and headed for the door. I got whacked in the cheek by someone's elbow. We streamed out and raced across the grass back towards the warm comfort of the orangery.

But then, halfway across the lawn, I stopped and turned around. I wanted to run, just like the others, but I didn't want to leave Imogen in the shed alone with Thomas. Though my heart was thumping hard, I took a deep breath and marched back across the lawn.

As I reached the shed I saw Thomas peering around behind it. Imogen huddled behind him, holding the lamp.

'Well,' Thomas said. 'If it isn't Crazy Jimmy himself.' He reached around and took hold of something, or someone, and hauled him out into the light. It was William D, of course, beside himself with glee at the trick.

'Where's William P?' I asked, taking his hand and leading him back to the house. I noticed there were quite a few leaves now, since the wind had picked up. Mike was going to have some work to do on Monday. I was pleased to see Thomas came with us, Imogen trundling along behind, scowling.

'He was too scared to come outside,' William D said.

'Did you wait until the scariest bit of the story before you banged on the shed?' Thomas asked.

William D nodded and I think Thomas was pretty impressed.

'But weren't you scared of the story too?' he asked.

'No,' William D said. 'I saw that story on *Real-Life Detectives*. I know what's on the car roof.'

'What?' Thomas asked.

'Just the boyfriend's head.'

On the way home, Daddy put his arm around Mummy. 'I'm glad you're not like Ellen,' he said. 'It's one of the things I love about you most, Polly. You're low-maintenance.'

'Not through choice, John,' Mummy said. 'Not through choice.'

I smiled as we walked past crowds of trick-or-treaters laughing and whooping. Glowing pumpkins lit three houses out of four on every street. Daisy and William D ran ahead shrieking with laughter at some private game. Maybe Imogen had a big house, maybe Imogen was pretty like Jasmine, maybe Imogen got to go to Barbados in the holidays. But just at that moment I wouldn't swap places with her for anything.

PART FOUR
November

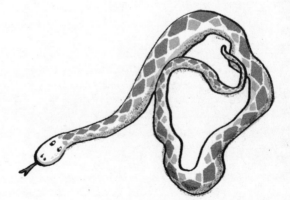

Behaviour Diary — William D.   Nov 11

I had to have a talk to William D
after observing his behaviour in the
playground. William D was insisting
people call him 'Crazy Jimmy,' and
chasing other pupils around, pretending
he was carrying a chainsaw.
Role play games are usually a very
healthy sign, but perhaps William D
is showing just a little too much
imagination?
We talked to the whole class
about respectful attitudes towards
mental health.

                              S. Duvall

Coming up for Air

'Why does my Mulberry handbag smell of vinegar?' Mummy said as we left the house on Saturday.

Daisy and I looked at each other then shrugged. We were on our way to the sports centre. We used to go to swimming lessons every Saturday morning but we weren't making a lot of progress so we stopped for a while. Mummy says the Deals are not natural swimmers. Daddy says nonsense and thinks we just need to be thrown in the deep end, but then William D fell in the Weyford Pond while he was collecting tadpoles and had to be rescued by Mr Campbell from our road, who happened to be walking past.

In the new term we've started up again. Because we had a break, we're a bit behind and we're all in with children much smaller than us which is a bit embarrassing, especially as Imogen is in the top group and sits smirking as she watches me try to get my arms out of the water. Hannah and Sophie from my class are also in Imogen's group, but they turn up later. Imogen has to come early because her little brother Casper is in my class. He's really good and zips past me but I don't mind because he's a sweet little boy and always says hello as he goes by.

I am making *some* progress, which is more than can be said for William D.

'Twenty-three swimming lessons,' Mummy says. 'And he still refuses to put his head under water.'

He just spends his whole time chatting to the other children in his group and trying to make the instructors laugh. He has his lesson first and I sit and watch him while Mummy chats with the other mummies. She often has to sit next to Ellen which she hates. This week Ellen was telling Mummy about Imogen's secondary school options. They're going to go private of course.

'Have you not considered Weyford Secondary School?' Mummy asked.

'Oh no,' Ellen said. 'Toby wouldn't let Imogen go there. Secondary is so important, don't you think?'

'I really like Haverford Ladies' Academy,' Imogen said. 'The school is in a former stately home. Ellen prefers Basfield School in Crompton though.'

'They have excellent stables,' Ellen explained. 'And they teach Business Studies and Deportment.'

'Chloe's going to Weyford,' Mummy said flatly. 'We're very excited about it.'

'Well, if that's the right school for you . . .' Ellen said, after a pause.

'Look at him now,' Mummy said, watching William D. 'He's going backwards.'

She was right. William D was holding a float in each hand and was kicking hard, but his feet were going all over the place and somehow he was getting further away from the wall. He grinned madly, clearly enjoying it, until he pushed down too hard on one of the floats and it slipped out and shot up into the air like a slice of toast. He went under and had to be rescued again.

'At least he got his head under water,' I said.

Mummy sighed.

Later on Emily and Tamsin came over for a play date. It's interesting watching Tamsin and Daisy play together. They're both really polite.

'Do you want to be Hermione?'

'No, no, you be Hermione, I insist.'

Or, 'Would you like to play a new game now?'

'Would you like to?'

'Only if it's OK with you.'

'Thank you, I would.'

Emily isn't like that at all. She tends to decide what game we play and even tells everyone else what to do and say. It's easier just to go along with her because she's so confident and in-charge. But sometimes I think it would be nice if she wasn't quite so bossy.

I like it when the four of us are together. We all get on very well even if Emily tries to boss everyone around and we spend a lot of time trying to stop Tamsin from climbing things. Her climbing was useful today though, because she went up the dessert apple tree and got the last ones, right up the top, which were nut-crunchy and delicious.

We played a massive game of Skink Hunt because the grass is nice and long. The weather was quite warm. I think sometimes summer days get lost in time and find themselves turning up in November or March by mistake, looking a bit embarrassed but determined to make the most of it and be lovely and hot anyway. So while we played, Daddy got the barbecue out and cooked us sausages and burgers for lunch. He sang a song about Emily as he pricked the sausages. It was to the tune of 'Shake it Off' by Taylor Swift, who he quite likes.

'Now the girls are gonna play, play, play, play, play
When Emmy comes to stay, stay, stay, stay, stay
Her name is Bella-may, may, may, may, may
Emily. Bellamy.'

Emily stared at him hard, then said, 'I don't like being called Emmy.'

Mummy says Emily gives 'withering stares'. Daddy certainly looked a bit withered. He sighed and flipped a burger.

Mummy came out with a tray of hot dog rolls and a salad, tripping over William D who had Minion goggles on and couldn't see where he was going. 'Where's Tamsin?' she asked, looking around.

'She's SkinkMaster,' I explained. 'She's supposed to be hiding until the Rollover Phase begins.'

'Then she has to sing the Song of Solitude,' Emily added. 'Before she can rejoin the game as a lowly sub-hunter.'

'Has Daddy been adding new rules to Skink Hunt again?' Mummy asked with a pained expression.

'Only a couple of new Phases,' Daddy said.

Builder's Tea

On Friday, at 7.32 a.m, Front Door chimed.

'I'll get it, I'll get it, I'll get it,' screeched William D. He raced out of the playroom, not wearing any pyjama bottoms. Mummy, who happened to be standing in the hall, had to leap back to avoid being run over. William D opened the letter box and peered through.

'It's not Charlie,' he said, disappointed.

'Why would Charlie be here at 7.32 a.m?' Mummy asked as she went to open Front Door. 'And put your pyjama bottoms on.' She yanked at the handle, but Front Door clearly didn't want to be opened.

'Sorry,' Mummy called out. 'The door's stuck, wait there.'

She went into the sitting room and we heard a lot of banging and thumping, then she reappeared in the hallway with Mr Peterson in tow. He frowned and inspected Front Door from the inside, shaking his head.

'Well that's the first job,' Mummy said. 'You'll need to sort Front Door out so you can get your tools in and out.'

But Mr Peterson was still shaking his head. He looked

glum. 'Problem's not with the door,' he said. 'You have a sagging lintel.'

'Well, I *am* forty-three,' Mummy said.

'No, I mean the brickwork over the top of the door is pressing down on the door itself. That's why it sticks.'

'That's fantastic!' Mummy said. 'That you've found the trouble, I mean. I'm so glad you're here finally.'

But Mr Peterson didn't look happy at all. 'It opened fine when I was here before,' he said.

Mummy shrugged. 'That's Front Door for you.'

'It'll be a big job to fix it,' Mr Peterson said, gloomily. 'Expensive.'

'It's all included in the quote though?' Mummy asked.

Mr Peterson nodded and sucked a lot of air through his teeth. He looked sadder than ever. As we finished breakfast, five builders came in one by one. Four men and one woman who had a big grin on her face and seemed to be the opposite of Mr Peterson. They managed to get Front Door open somehow, despite the sagging lintel, and started carrying in boxes of tools and pieces of machinery.

'Hello,' Mummy said to each one as he or she came in.

We made them all a cup of tea. I had the job of finding out how they all took it.

'*How* many sugars?' I asked Piotr incredulously.

'Four,' he repeated, holding up four fingers to make sure I understood.

We wrote down everything on a big piece of paper and stuck it up on the fridge. Mummy said we were going to be making a lot of tea over the next few weeks.

'They don't speak much English,' Mr Peterson explained as everyone slurped their tea and grinned at each other in the sitting room. But then he pointed to one man with a leather tool belt. 'Except that one – Karl. He's Polish.'

'Put your shoes on,' Mummy said to William D as he wandered past. He now had pants on, at least. He ignored her and went upstairs. 'Are they all Polish?' she asked Mr Peterson.

'No. Karl is the only one. Those two are Romanian and the girl, Ana, is from Slovakia.' Ana waved at the sound of her name. She seemed nice. 'Karl speaks a bit of German,' Mr Peterson went on. 'And Ana speaks German and Romanian so they all pass on my instructions. It's a bit like Chinese Whispers but we muddle through.'

Karl and Piotr finished their tea and handed me their cups with a grin before going upstairs to have a look around.

'What about the other chap?' Mummy asked, indicating a short man with black curly hair and no teeth. 'Where's he from?'

'We don't know,' Mr Peterson said with a sigh. 'No one speaks his language. But he's good with bricks.'

The man with no name and no country grinned at us toothlessly. We all grinned back.

Ana noticed all the patches of nearly-white paint on the walls and started pointing at them one by one. 'Nice,' she said. 'Not nice. Very not nice.'

'Have you decided on a colour yet?' Mr Peterson asked Mummy.

'Very nearly,' Mummy said. 'I've narrowed it down to five. Or six.'

Someone started hammering something upstairs.

'It's started,' Mummy said.

But Mr Peterson looked alarmed. 'Who's up there? We're not supposed to start hammering until eight,' he said. 'Let me go and sort it out. I think Piotr is still on European time.'

But it turned out that it was William D who was doing the banging. He'd found a hammer and was whacking the sticky-up nails on the first-floor landing.

'PUT YOUR SHOES ON!' Mummy yelled as he came down, grinning from ear to ear.

'Things are going to be a bit mad around the house for the next few weeks,' Mummy said once we'd finally left the house and were walking to school.

'Even madder than usual?' Daisy asked.

'Yes, Daisy,' Mummy said. 'Even madder than usual.'

Sleepover?

William D has three stars on his star chart. He was staring at them, frowning, on Saturday morning when I came downstairs for breakfast. He looked up at the top of the fridge where Mummy keeps the packet of star stickers.

'Chloe, can you help me get more stars?' he asked.

'Yes, OK, William D,' I said. 'Tell you what. Let's get breakfast organised and wash up afterwards. Then we'll tidy up the playroom together and go outside to play instead of watching telly. Mummy will definitely give you a star if you do all that.'

William D stared at me as if I was a crazy person.

'I mean help me get the stickers down off the top of the fridge,' he explained.

At swimming later that morning, we sat watching as Gabi tried and failed to get William D to put his head under water. When Mummy wasn't watching, Gabi briskly ducked his head under. He came up spluttering and looking outraged.

'How are you getting on with the renovations?' Ellen asked Mummy.

'Brilliant, brilliant,' Mummy said. 'Mr Peterson says he's very nearly ready to start.'

'I thought they'd already started?'

'That was the plan. Mr Peterson said they needed to sort out the lintel above Front Door first, but then they discovered some rising damp which needed to be fixed before they could start on the lintel, then they realised they were going to need to re-lay the damp course before they started on the rising damp, then they found the damp was from a leaking pipe, so they decided they needed to replace some pipes before they did anything else, then they had to dig up some concrete that was laid over the pipes they needed to replace, then . . . oh, who knows what else. I'm not sure they've even *found* the start yet, let alone started on it.'

'Well, let me know if you want the number of *our* builder,' Ellen said. 'He's working on David Walliams' London flat at the moment but I think he's free early next year.'

'Thanks,' Mummy said. 'But he might be slightly out of our price range.'

'You get what you pay for,' Ellen said. 'By the way, Imogen has been asking if she can go for a sleepover with Chloe.'

My ears pricked up at this.

'Has she?' Mummy asked in surprise. She dropped her voice so I had to lean across to hear her. 'I didn't know the girls were . . . close.'

'I know they've had their differences,' Ellen said quietly. 'But now they're in the play together, I know Imogen wants to work hard to build friendships with everyone. We talked about her being more forgiving.'

My face grew hot. The way Ellen was talking made it seem like Imogen was being the big-hearted one, trying to be friendly to me after I'd been horrible. What did she mean about being more forgiving? Forgiving what?

Mummy and I talked about it in the car on the way home. I told her that I was willing to give it a try. I didn't want to seem like the one who was being mean.

But I had my doubts.

Cannon to the Left of Them

On Wednesday at the play rehearsal, Daisy and I went to talk to Mr Bolli to tell him about Daisy not wanting to be a palace guard and ask whether there was another job she could do, offstage. He nodded and had a think. Then he clapped his hands together.

'Got it! We need a prompt-a,' he said.

'A promper?' Daisy said, puzzled.

'Not a promper,' Mr Bolli said, rolling his eyes. 'Listen. A prompt-a'

'A prompt,' I said, translating. 'A prompt is someone who sits just off stage and calls out lines to the actors if they forget them.'

Daisy's face lit up. 'That sounds perfect!' she said.

Mr Bolli blinked in surprise. 'Madame Adams will be happy because she was going to have to do it. No one else wanted to. Are you sure you want to be a prompt-a?'

'I'm sure,' Daisy said, nodding firmly.

So Daisy was asked to read through the whole script and get really familiar with it. This will be a big help

153

for me because it means she can play all the other characters in my scenes when we're rehearsing.

Mr Coleman is not happy about the building work. He came around in the evening after the workmen had gone.

'I told you about it,' Mummy said to him through the window. She hadn't tried to open Front Door, she always says there are certain people she prefers talking to out of the window and Mr Coleman was definitely one of them. 'We knocked on everyone's door and sent an email and put up planning permission notices and everything. What else could we have done? Sent a carrier pigeon?'

'You said you were having "a little work done,"' Mr Coleman replied. 'It sounds like you're burrowing down to the centre of the earth.'

'Oh, it hasn't been that bad.'

'The whole building has been shaking all day. It sounds like they're setting off cannon.'

'They're from Eastern Europe,' Mummy explained. 'They do things with gusto there. I'm sure they'll settle down in the coming weeks.'

'Weeks!' Mr Coleman shrieked. 'How long is this expected to go on for?'

'We'll be finished by Christmas,' Mummy said.

Mr Coleman stormed off, his bald head bright pink.

Mummy turned to me and scrunched her chin. 'I really hope they're finished by Christmas.'

Mr Peterson had already found lots of other things

that needed fixing before he could fix the things he needed to fix before he could do the decorating.

'He's not very happy about it,' Mummy said.

'He's never very happy,' I pointed out. 'Does this mean it's going to cost us even more money?'

'No,' Mummy replied with a mischievous grin. 'Because he's already told me how much the job is going to cost, anything else which turns up he needs to pay for.'

'Oh, that's good,' I said.

'Well, yes,' Mummy replied. 'Except it might mean the job will take longer. It might not be finished by Christmas. And that, Chloe Deal, would be the disaster to end all disasters.'

I nodded.

'By the way,' Mummy said. 'Do you know what you want for Christmas?'

'Nothing really,' I said. 'A book?'

'Is that all? There must be something else?'

'I'll have a think,' I said.

The truth was that I didn't want to ask for anything too expensive because asking for expensive things is what has made Daddy have to go and work in Germany. The more we ask for, the longer he'll have to work there. All I really want for Christmas is to have Daddy back.

Girl Talk!

On Saturday Imogen came for her sleepover. Ellen was craning her neck the whole time she was in the house, trying to see up the stairs and peeking into different rooms to look at the décor. Mummy didn't seem to want to show her round the house and kept her in the hall. They spent a long time talking about the various colour patches on the walls. Mummy was currently favouring Somnolent Lily but Ellen seemed to like Natural Hush.

I was a bit nervous about the sleepover. Imogen had been my enemy for so long. Or at least my frenemy. Could we now be friends? Was it that easy? Mummy had told me to be nice. Anyway, as they stood chatting she and Ellen were both cracking jokes and I thought if they can do it then so can I.

First of all I took Imogen for a tour of the house. A lot of it was warnings.

'Best to avoid that step. Watch out for nails there,' I said. 'Mind the flappy wallpaper. That light switch sometimes doesn't work. And when it does it gives you a shock.'

Imogen was a bit spooked by the haunted landing on

the second floor. Even though I explained that there wasn't actually a ghost in the spare room like Daisy and I had thought at one point, the landing was still dark because the lights didn't work. The floorboards were especially creaky in that hallway and the wallpaper was especially flappy. That's all quite spooky enough even without a ghost, frankly.

Imogen shivered as she walked along. We went upstairs to the top floor.

'You sleep in here?' Imogen asked when I showed her my attic room. She shivered again and I kicked the radiator which sometimes gets it going. It burped and rattled into action.

'Yes, it's cosy, and I like what I can see out of the window.'

'But there's a bigger room downstairs? The one with the skeleton painting on the wall?'

'I prefer this one. I can hear the bats when they're nesting.'

'You have bats?' she said, sounding horrified.

I explained about the horseshoe bats in the loft and how they were actually very sweet and how we'd had to leave them alone until they'd finished breeding but then somehow Daddy hadn't got around to blocking up the hole they came in and out of and we'd decided to let them stay.

'They're part of the family now,' I finished.

'Like the Addams Family,' Imogen suggested.

'No, like our family,' I said firmly.

Imogen was amazed by my big bookshelf stuffed with paperbacks.

'Have you read all of these?' she asked.

'No,' I said, which was true. I'd read almost all of them but there were a few Malory Towers books I hadn't read, and maybe a dog-eared copy of *Swallows and Amazons* I hadn't got around to. Plus there was my TBR pile which had seven books in it.

'No, I didn't think so,' Imogen sniffed. 'You should get a Kindle, then you can get rid of all of these. You can fit all the books in the world on one little Kindle.'

'I don't want all the books in the world,' I said. 'I just want my books. And I like to be able to see them.'

After that we went downstairs and I showed her the garden. She seemed astonished to see long grass and all the bushes and flowers growing a bit wild. She stepped on a rotten apple and squealed.

'Your gardener should really pick these up,' she said.

'He's very busy,' I replied, looking over at Daddy who was sitting in a deckchair reading a book and sipping a cup of coffee. 'So what do you think of the house?'

Imogen thought for a bit. 'It's sweet,' she said. 'All tumbledown and rustic. Like Miss Honey's cottage.'

'Miss Honey's cottage doesn't have electricity,' I pointed out. 'We have electricity. In most rooms.'

'No, I like it,' Imogen said. 'Our house is so neat and tidy and well-maintained and pretty. So it's nice to see a house that's . . . different.' With that she picked her way daintily back through the damp grass towards the house.

Even when Imogen is trying to be nice she somehow manages to be mean. The things she says about our house compared to their house are true, and are the same reasons I prefer our house. But it's the way she says the things that counts.

At dinner Imogen studied her food very carefully.

'Are these Armenian carrots?'

'I don't know,' Mummy said. 'I got them from Lidl.'

'And what's this bread?'

'Again, it's Lidl.'

'I prefer farmhouse bread.'

'Sorry, we don't have any of that.'

Imogen speared a sausage on her fork and inspected it. 'What are these sausages?' she asked.

'Once more, Lidl,' Mummy replied. 'I can save you a lot of time by informing you that it's all Lidl.'

'They're not that Lidl,' Daisy and I chorused. 'They're actually quite big!'

This is a favourite joke in our house and we fell about. But not Imogen. She just looked at us, mystified.

'But where did you buy them?' she asked Mummy.

'Lidl,' Mummy repeated. 'It's a supermarket. Off the Guildford Road. Next to the crematorium.'

'Oh, I don't think I've been there,' Imogen said.

'Where does your mummy get sausages?' Mummy asked.

'Ellen orders them online,' Imogen said. 'Artisansausages.com.'

'Of course,' Mummy said. 'I have it bookmarked.'

'Can we have artisan sausages?' William D asked. He loves sausages, William D does. 'What's artisan?'

'We can have something even better,' Mummy said. 'I'll ask Daddy to bring back some German sausages from Eindhoven.'

'German sausages?' William D asked. 'Is that a thing?'

'Of *course* it's a thing!' Mummy cried. 'Germany is the Land of Sausages.'

William D's eyes lit up at the prospect. Imogen stopped talking for a bit and got on with eating her non-Artisan sausages. Mummy gave me a wink.

My mummy is amazing.

Girl Offline

After dinner we watched a DVD and then went up to my room. Imogen suggested we should give each other a makeover which I didn't really want to do but I went along with it.

'Where's your make-up?' Imogen asked, looking around.

'I don't have any,' I said.

She looked at me and sniffed.

'We could ask Mummy if we could borrow some of her make-up?'

Imogen screwed up her nose and shook her head. 'She gets her eyeliner from Boots. Don't you watch Zoella?'

'No, we don't have Sky.'

'She's not on telly!' Imogen shrieked. 'On YouTube.'

I shrugged. I knew Daisy sometimes watched Zoella but I'd thought she was watching old TV shows.

'I've brought a couple of things,' she said, kneeling down and opening up her case.

Imogen's make-up bag filled about two thirds of the

case. She lifted it out with difficulty and unzipped the bag, rolling it out like she was a safe-cracker. She looked up at me, then back down at the make-up. Then back up at me.

'Let's get started,' she said. 'Lots to do.'

It turns out it takes AGES to do make-up. You've got to put on foundation, then lipstick, then blusher, then eyeliner, then some other things I can't remember. We did our toenails too, which was the bit I liked the best. I found it really funny but Imogen seemed to take it very seriously. Daisy came in after a bit and her eyes lit up when she saw what we were doing. She likes this sort of stuff, and she joined in and chatted with Imogen about different brands of make-up and we looked at YouTubers who seemed to spend all their time putting on make-up then showing you the best way to take the make-up off, which seemed to take even longer. Honestly, why put it on at all? Then you don't have to mess about with cotton wool and nail polish remover.

Anyway, it was sort of fun and we all took photos of each other pouting and trying to look like pop stars. But I insisted we take it all off afterwards.

Mummy had brought in a blow-up mattress for me to sleep on and at lights out we lay in bed and chatted about school, and the play, and swimming and Christmas and boys and how cold my room was, and make-up and films and songs and all sorts of things. In the dark, when you can't see the other person's face, it's easier to talk about some things.

'In the play,' I said eventually. 'In the scene with you and Aladdin, in the cave . . .'

'Yes?'

'Are you going to . . . are you and Thomas going to . . . ?'

'Going to what, Chloe?' she asked.

'Going to kiss?' I asked.

'Why?' she asked. 'Would you be jealous?'

'NO!' I said, perhaps a little too loudly.

'Because a stage kiss doesn't mean anything, Chloe,' she said. 'You have to kiss all sorts of people, when you're an actor. You just have to be professional.'

'I suppose so,' I said.

'You do like him a bit don't you?' Imogen said after a moment.

I hesitated, but then said, 'Yes.'

Then we both giggled.

It felt dangerous to say it out loud but thrilling too. Just as I was about to drop off to sleep I thought that maybe Imogen wasn't so bad after all. We liked some different things and maybe we weren't ever going to be BFFs, but it's good to know people who are a bit different.

In the morning Toby came to collect Imogen. When Mummy offered him a cup of tea he said yes. He was wearing aftershave and had his top button undone.

163

'John not here?' he asked, looking around. 'I heard he was working in Germany?'

'He is, but he comes back for weekends. He's just at Home 'n Garden Megastore at the moment.'

'You must get lonely during the week,' Toby said.

'Not really,' Mummy said. 'You're never alone when you have four children.'

'You really don't look old enough to have four children,' Toby said, before sipping his tea.

'Nonetheless . . .' Mummy said.

'Chloe,' Imogen said, interrupting this interesting exchange. 'I keep forgetting to mention that I'm planning a read-through of the *Aladdin* script for all the key parts on Thursday, we'll do it in the summerhouse. Can you come?'

I looked at Mummy and she nodded.

'Sounds brilliant,' I said to my new friend.

The Magic Carpet

Next Thursday after school, Emily and I walked together to Imogen's house for the read-through. As we walked I saw Tobias up ahead, being pulled along by his mummy. She stopped and turned to say something to him. She looked tired, like Daddy does when he gets back from Germany on Friday nights.

Emily started to say something but I interrupted her.

'Hold on, Emily. I have an idea.' I ran up to Tobias and his mother.

When we got to Imogen's house we walked around the side and down to the summerhouse. I was excited to be going. Everyone had been talking about it all day at school. We were going to have biscuits and hot chocolate and there weren't going to be any grown-ups. I was still a little bit unsure about Imogen, but it was nice of her to invite me. Maybe she was changing. The garden looked even bigger in the daylight.

The grass was all neatly cut in strips and there were sharp edges to the flower beds. It didn't look like a good garden for Skink Hunt. There would be nowhere for the

Skink to regenerate during the Dimension Phases. Everyone looked up as we came in.

'What's HE doing here?' Imogen asked, pointing at Tobias who was grinning in delight.

'I invited him,' I said. 'Sorry, I should have checked with you. But he does have three lines and you said this read-through was for everyone with lines.'

Imogen didn't say anything else about it just then, but I could tell she was furious with me. I felt a bit bad about it, actually. I honestly hadn't meant to annoy Imogen just when we were starting to get on better. But on the other hand, I didn't think it was such a rude thing for me to have done. Tobias DID need to be there. I was completely sure about that.

We started reading and got about halfway through the script. Tobias was very fidgety. He finds it hard to sit still for long and the carpet doesn't have a very active role in the first few scenes. So I gave him my phone to look at and poked him when it was his turn to do a line. His first one was 'Climb aboard!' When it was time for him to deliver it, he leapt up and collapsed flat on the wooden floor of the summerhouse.

'CLIMB ABOARD!' he shouted at the top of his voice. Everyone laughed, except for Imogen, who glared at him. Then she realised I was watching her so she changed her expression to a smile.

Surprise!

Daddy was up when I came downstairs on Saturday morning. He picked me up and spun me around the kitchen. I squeezed him tight and breathed in his Daddy smell. I let him make me toast for breakfast, even though he doesn't spread the butter right to the crusts which is how I like it.

While he was doing that, Clematis brought in a dead shrew, which I don't think we've had before. I put it in a bowl, meaning to go and put it in the bins when I had my shoes on. My phone pinged and I saw I had a text from Emily asking if I wanted to do something. I texted back to see if she wanted to come over for a game of Skink Hunt. Long grass is no good for playing BOOMBall but provides good ground cover for Skink Hunt.

Daddy stood at the Aga and sipped coffee as I ate my toast and Observed him. He looked tired. Germany was taking it out of him. I wanted to ask him to play Skink Hunt with us today but I thought maybe he would just want to rest. William D had already eaten his breakfast and was now watching TV very loudly in the playroom. Daisy came down, her hair all messy, and asked for Fruit

Hoops. Daddy yawned and poured some into a bowl on the table, sloshed in some milk and slapped a spoon down for her. Mummy appeared and gave me and Daisy a kiss. Mummy looked half asleep as well. I don't think she sleeps well when Daddy's not here.

'I just can't seem to wake up today,' she said, stretching.

'What's this?' Daisy asked, sliding something around in her bowl.

Mummy peered at it before letting out a shriek.

'It's a mouse!' she yelled. 'How did a mouse get into your cereal?' She leapt back from the table, slipped and fell over. Mummy HATES dead animals.

'It's a shrew, actually,' I said. 'And I think I might have accidentally put it there.'

Mummy glared at me. Well, at least she was fully awake now.

Emily didn't answer my text for ages. She doesn't check her phone very often. So I popped over the road to her house after lunch and knocked on the door. Vicky answered.

'Emily's not here, poppet,' she said. 'She's at Imogen's for a play date.'

Since when have Emily and Imogen been friends? I thought as I went back home. I checked AppChat. Emily's avatar picture is so her. It's a picture of her with a grumpy face on. I went back home and didn't think anything more about it until much later when I

168

saw Emily coming home with her mummy. She'd clearly just come from Imogen's house, because she was wearing make-up. And a dress! My jaw dropped. Emily? Wearing a dress? What was going on? Emily was *my* friend – she'd never liked Imogen. She hated wearing dresses even more than I did. I logged on to AppChat. There was the usual argument going on about who had started this chat. I saw Imogen was logged on.

I wrote a public message but tagged Imogen. 'Enjoy your makeover session?'

She replied. 'Yes! Brilliant fun!'

Then she sent another public message. 'Remember this?'

She'd attached a new photo. It took me a moment to recognise that it was me! Imogen had shared the picture of me from the sleepover when I was pouting. I remembered she'd told me to look like Ariana Grande and I had this stupid serious face on. It had all been a joke but now it looked like I was really trying hard.

Lots of people made comments like 'lolz' and 'I've never seen Chloe wearing a dress B4.'

Imogen wrote: 'I bet Thomas would like to see this lol!'

I gasped. I knew I shouldn't have told her that I liked Thomas. Now everyone knew. And then a new message popped up from Emily.

'She thinks she's Ariana! ☺'

Well that was rich coming from her. I was going to write something rude back but decided against it – I'd see her at school tomorrow.

Then she'd have some explaining to do.

I didn't see Emily until lunchtime, because William D wouldn't put his shoes on and so made us all late and we had to race right into school. Some of the other girls were giggling as I passed them in the classroom going to my seat. I think Sophie whispered 'Here's Ariana!' and Imogen tried to look all innocent. When I finally caught up with Emily I was really cross.

'Why did you make that comment about me on AppChat?' I said, launching right into it.

'What comment?' she asked.

'You said I thought I was Ariana Grande!' I said. I think there might have been some other people watching this exchange.

Emily frowned. 'You *were* trying to look like Ariana Grande,' she said. 'It was just a joke.'

'I expect it from the others, that they'd tease me,' I said. 'But not you. Anyway, I saw you yesterday, coming home from Imogen's, wearing make-up. Wearing a DRESS!' I was so angry. It was so unfair of Emily to tease me for doing something that she'd done too. She just looked back at me, scowling as girls surrounded us, whispering and laughing.

'You're being really mean,' she said, quietly.

'What do you care? You have your new bestie Imogen now,' I said, then I turned and walked away. I didn't need her. I didn't need anyone.

I hate Imogen!

I knew she was being fake when she pretended to be my friend. I know she's trying to get back at me because I brought Tobias to her house for the rehearsal. I also felt bad about what I'd said to Emily. It wasn't her fault. It was Imogen's fault. I lay in bed for ages last night thinking about how awful she was. In the morning I was exhausted and didn't want to get up. My room was freezing so I ovenned a bit to warm myself and fumed about how unfair it all was.

Mummy called for me three times before she came up.

'What's wrong, sweetie?' she asked as I popped my head out from under the covers. 'You're all red. Have you been crying?'

I shook my head.

'Did you have a bad dream? Is it something at school?' I was about to tell her about Imogen, but it was really embarrassing and then I remembered Mummy and Ellen were friends now and I decided not to say anything. I shook my head.

'I'm just not feeling very well,' I said.

Mummy felt my head. 'You do feel a bit hot,' she said.

That was probably because I'd been ovenning, but I didn't let on.

'You'd better stay at home today. I'll call Declan and tell him I can't come in. Do you feel up to coming down for breakfast?'

'In a bit,' I said. I was actually ravenously hungry and already starting to feel guilty about lying to Mummy.

'OK,' she said. 'Come down if you think you're up to it.'

She stopped in the doorway and shivered. 'It is really cold in here. I can't wait until we can move you into your proper room.' Then she shut the door and I groaned.

I waited a few minutes, then wandered downstairs. Daisy and William D were in their school uniforms, eating breakfast at the table in the kitchen.

'She's not ill,' William D said pointing a milky spoon at me accusingly.

'I'm sorry you're not feeling well,' Daisy said and got up to give me a hug.

I'm not sure which was worse. Being accused of lying by William D or getting a hug from Daisy even though I wasn't really ill. I ate a little bit of cereal, pretending I was forcing it down, even though I wanted to eat everything in the fridge.

'Will you be OK here on your own while I drop William D down at the school?' Mummy asked.

Lately she's been letting me stay in the house on my

own for short times while she pops to the shops or goes off to pick someone up. It's brilliant being in the house on my own, and also a little scary. I nodded.

Daisy gave me another hug as she left to walk to school on her own. Suddenly I wanted to tell her to wait so I could run upstairs and get into my uniform. I watched her out of the sitting-room window as she trotted off down York Road, plaits waving about and her big school bag bumping against her bottom. My breath frosted against the glass and as I wiped it, I saw Emily come out of her house with her mummy. I glared at her but she didn't look up.

When Mummy and William D had gone, I went back up to my room and read a book in bed to keep warm. I'm reading *I Capture the Castle* at the moment and it's really good. I think I might have dozed off because the next thing I knew was that Front Door had banged and there was the sound of children downstairs. Could the others be back already?

I got up and stepped lightly to the bannisters. I heard William D shrieking and the sound of some other little boys. What was going on? I went down, remembering to look wan, and came upon a scene of chaos. Five boys, including William D, were charging around the house hitting each other with their school bags. I counted three Williams, a Zach and a Max. Mummy was sitting halfway up the stairs watching with horror. I came and sat beside her.

'How are you feeling?' she asked.

'A bit better,' I said. 'I had a snooze. Why are there lots of boys here?'

'The boiler was broken at St Andrew's,' she said. 'They had to close the school. I made the mistake of saying I was taking the day off to look after you and everyone asked if I could look after their children too.'

'You said yes?' I asked, surprised.

'I could hardly say no,' Mummy replied. 'I was there in my cardigan and wellies. Four other mums were dressed in business suits, on their way to the train station.'

The boys were already running amok. Max went into the sitting room and came back out with the poker from the fire companion set. William H crashed into the phone table, sending the cordless handset skittering across the hall floor. Zach had found a walking stick and was being Darth Maul whacking the other boys with both ends.

'But they'll owe me after this,' Mummy said grimly. 'Oh, how they'll owe me.'

William D tripped Zach up, sending him and the walking stick clattering to the floor.

'Awkward!' William D yelled triumphantly.

This was my fault, I thought. For pretending to be ill. If I hadn't done that then Mummy would have been dressed for work too and someone else would have been stuck with five energetic boys.

'Oh no,' Mummy said, holding her head.

174

'What's wrong?'

'I've just realised I'm going to need to go to the supermarket. I don't have any food in the house at all. Five boys are going to need a mountain of food. I'll have to take them with me.'

'Can I stay here?' I asked as Max and William P started sword fighting with a walking stick and the poker from the fire.

'I could do with your help, if you think you can manage it?' she asked.

I was about to say no, but I felt guilty already for lying about being ill. I couldn't leave Mummy to face the supermarket all on her own with five little monsters.

'OK, Mummy,' I said bravely. 'I'll come.'

William P tackled William D and sent him thudding into the wall. A shower of plaster fell from the cracked ceiling. William D roared and shoved William P back and into the opposite wall while Mummy and I watched in alarm. A picture of Daisy in her school uniform fell down and the glass shattered. Mummy sighed.

Can I Help You, Madame?

'Now everyone listen. LISTEN!' Mummy screeched outside Sainsbury's.

The boys raced around her like little planets orbiting the sun, crashing into each other. Passing shoppers gave us a wide berth.

'When we get inside, I need you all to stay close to me and Chloe. Don't go running off, I won't be able to keep track of you and you might get taken away by Bad Pixies.'

The Bad Pixies thing was something she'd invented to stop us from running off in supermarkets. It had worked on me and Daisy but it doesn't work at all with William D. He told me he WANTS to find the Bad Pixies and 'take them down'. In any case the boys didn't listen and ran off in all directions as soon as we got inside. I saw the manager look up in horror as they raced in, shouting and trying to trip each other up.

Mummy refused to meet his gaze and muttered to me, 'Let's just get this done as quickly as possible and get

176

home. I'll try and chase them down just so I can keep an eye on them. You get all the things on this shopping list.'

'I can chase them if you like?' I suggested.

'No,' she said, 'You're not well. I already feel bad about dragging you out here.'

So then I felt bad about making her feel bad about dragging me here. I took the shopping list and went around the supermarket grabbing things and dropping them in the trolley. Bananas, grapes, blueberries, sliced ham, sliced chicken, lettuce, margarine, mayonnaise, dishwasher tablets, frozen pizza for our dinner. From time to time a boy or two would hurtle past, sometimes with Mummy in hot pursuit, puffing and panting.

'Hurry, Chloe, hurry!' Mummy shouted on one of these encounters, and I scurried along as quickly as I could.

The shop alarm went off at one point, which was almost certainly William D. It stopped blaring just as I grabbed the last item, a bag of dry cat food. Then I raced to the checkouts where the manager had opened a new lane just for us. He ran everything through at lightning speed and Mummy timed it perfectly, skidding up with her card and feeding it into the reader. She had a hold of Max, who's probably the most destructive of all the boys. He was fighting to escape as Mummy tapped in her pin.

'I'm sorry, Madame, that card has been declined,' the manager said.

'What?' Mummy replied. 'I must have put the wrong PIN in. STAND STILL, MAX!'

'No it's the right PIN, but there are *insufficient funds*,' the manager said, leaning in towards Mummy and whispering.

Mummy turned red. Then she took out another card. 'Try this one,' she said. 'But wait. Can I first put some things back?'

The manager nodded.

Mummy put back the dishwasher tablets, the sliced chicken, the mayonnaise and the blueberries. This time, the card worked and we all sighed with relief. The manager more than anyone.

Then the tricky bit started. We had to round up the rest of the boys and convince them to come with us back to the car. It took AGES. The manager helped – I think he might have been keen for us to leave the shop. We had four of them but couldn't find Max, who had escaped again. The manager discovered him eventually, hiding underneath the World Foods shelf and he was really dusty when we dragged him out.

When we got them back into the car I said to Mummy, 'Do you know, I don't think William D is all that naughty. Not when you compare him to some other boys.'

'I agree,' she replied, watching William P in the mirror. He was picking his nose and wiping it on the car window.

Eventually we were home and Mummy spent the next hour making sandwiches while the boys tore up the

178

garden. I saw Mr Coleman poke his head over the fence with a cross look on his face. Mummy and I watched as he shouted something at the boys. William P stuck out his bottom and waggled it at Mr Coleman.

'Good for you, William P,' Mummy muttered. 'Now, Chloe. There isn't much ham or mayonnaise, so is it OK if you have a cheese and pickle sandwich instead?'

'OK,' I said. 'What are you going to have?'

'I'll just have some celery,' she said. 'FHB, remember?'

Family Hold Back. That meant there wasn't enough. 'I'll just have celery too,' I said. If I hadn't pretended to be ill, I'd be having a hot school dinner right now. Mummy could have eaten my cheese and pickle sandwich.

'No,' she said. 'You have to eat something. Feed a cold, starve a fever and all that.'

She opened the kitchen door, letting in a blast of freezing air and called for the boys to come in for lunch. They nearly trampled her, racing in, fighting to be first. Zachary was all wrapped up in the bunting from the secret garden, William P was hitting William H with a tomato cane. I took my sandwich and sat on the counter to get out of their way. They were like gannets, jamming the sandwiches into their mouths, gulping down great drafts of squash while Mummy watched, wide-eyed. She usually struggles to get William D to eat much, but today he was stuffing his face along with the rest of them.

'I thought we had more money now Daddy was working in Germany,' I said.

Mummy looked at me and smiled. 'We do, sweetie. But most of it is going on the house. Once we get that finished and have paid everything to Mr Peterson, then there'll be more for other things. Like food. I promise.'

'I don't want food,' I said as she rummaged in the fridge. 'Not if it means Daddy has to keep going to Germany.'

'So you don't want any of this German sausage in a sandwich?' she asked holding up some bratwurst she'd found at the back.

'Well, maybe just a small one,' I said.

Mummy said, 'Who wants more?' They all wanted more, and Mummy really struggled to find things. They ate all the cheese and every last crumb of bread. Mummy found some old ice cream in the big freezer and that finished them off. One by one they went back outside. Mummy sighed with relief as the last boy, Zach, finally announced he was full.

'Did you enjoy that?' Mummy asked, taking Zach's empty bowl away.

'Yes,' he said, before burping loudly. Then he looked at Mummy curiously. 'Who are you?' he asked.

'I'm William D's mummy,' Mummy explained.

'OK,' he said, satisfied, and ran back outside to join the others.

Jacob's Deal

A short play by Chloe Deal

Int: Kitchen. Evening. Daisy and Chloe are doing homework at kitchen table. Mummy is inspecting a paint colours brochure. Jacob is standing, staring into the open fridge. His beard is long and whiskery. William D enters stage left and approaches Mummy.

William D: Are you thinking what I'm thinking?

Mummy: I doubt it.

William D: Are you sure?

Mummy: Hmmm, let me guess, you were thinking about the Playbox IV?

William D: See, you WERE thinking what I was thinking.

Mummy: That reminds me, girls, have you thought of what you want for Christmas?

Daisy: A phone.

Chloe: Um, socks?

Mummy: Daisy, you might need to lower your expectations slightly. Chloe, you can raise yours a little.

SFX: 'Bang Bang,' by Jessie J, plays.

It is Jacob's phone. He yanks it eagerly out of his pocket and reads the screen. He frowns and leaves the room.

Chloe: (to Daisy) That was interesting.

Daisy: What was interesting?

Chloe: 'Bang Bang' by Jessie J.

Daisy: What about it?

Chloe: That's Charlie's tune.

Chloe runs after Jacob and catches him at the bottom of the stairs.

Chloe: Jacob, stop!

Jacob: (stopping) Hi, Chloe.

Chloe: Your beard's looking good. And is that a new jacket?

Jacob: Thanks. (beams) I got it at . . .

(Suddenly sensing something is going on, he stops talking and eyes Chloe suspiciously.)

What do you want?

Chloe: Do you remember when I gave you that phone credit, and you said you owed me?

Jacob: (slowly) Yes . . .

Chloe: Well, do you think you could help me and Daisy with something, in return?

Jacob: Help you with what?

Chloe: Are you busy tomorrow night?

Back to School

I went back to school the next day, gratefully, and I decided I would never to pretend to be ill again. It causes too many problems. I was a bit nervous about going back in but everyone seemed to have forgotten about the photos. Things move on quickly, but Emily and I avoided each other.

I was pleased to be back because after school we had a two-hour rehearsal for the play. The idea was that we'd run through the whole thing for the first time. Imogen was taking it very seriously. When I got to the hall she was there already, wearing her dancing gear, with a loose top and skirt over stretchy Lycra leggings. She had her hair all tied up in a ponytail and had put lip-gloss on and was doing stretching exercises. I was just wearing my school uniform. I hadn't thought to change. Some other people had changed into comfortable clothes but most of us were in uniform.

So we started the read through, trying to put ourselves in the right positions as we went through the scenes. It took ages. No one knew their lines and just read from the script, head down. Daisy kept having to prompt people when it was their turn.

'Put-a some life into it,' Mr Bolli cried. 'You're not reading a eulogy.'

Oliver was just the worst. The understudies were asked to do a scene and he didn't know any of his lines and just read from the script the whole time and still got it wrong by reading the stage directions out loud. Madame Adams got cross. Then later he went missing for a while and Daisy had to read all his lines. He turned up again eventually and explained he'd got hungry and had gone off to get a Mars bar from his bag.

When I was reading my lines it was hard to imagine how it would be on the night. No one was in the right position. The back drops weren't painted and the stage crew were wandering back and forth carrying pieces of palace or lighting equipment. Tamsin dropped a microphone stand on her foot and had to go and sit down for a few minutes.

There's another bit in the play when me and my men are searching through big clay jars and baskets in the marketplace looking for Aladdin and Jasmine, where Aladdin pops out of a basket and throws a snake towards me. I have to catch it, then look at it in horror before throwing it into the crowd, which is supposed to get a big laugh. Unfortunately when we practised it I kept dropping the snake. It made it worse that it was Thomas throwing it to me. I didn't want to look completely rubbish in front of him and that just made it even harder. We tried it a few times and the more I dropped it the

184

more nervous I got and the more I dropped it the next time. Eventually Madame Adams said we should just move on, but that I was to practise catching snakes in my own time.

I enjoyed the read-through, and tried to put as much variation and personality into my voice as I could. But I made sure it was MY voice. I didn't put on an accent. I didn't try to go deep or anything. I saw Mr Bolli nodding at me encouragingly. But I felt very self-conscious about doing all the gestures and the expressions and the 'stage-dancing' that helped me remember my lines. No one else was doing that sort of thing. Also, I was a bit worried about the bit when Aladdin kisses Jasmine. It happens near the end. I knew it was just a run-through, but Imogen was standing right next to Thomas and I wondered if she might lean over and kiss him on the cheek, or maybe they'd both just giggle and he would blush which would mean that he liked her.

So when the moment came, I was coiled tighter than a spring. The scene is set in a flooded cave and, with waters rising, Aladdin takes the opportunity to hug and kiss Jasmine.

'The water is rising, Aladdin, there's nowhere to go,' Imogen said in a panicked voice.

'Do you think you can swim back the way we came?' Thomas said.

'No, it's too far, and the Vizier's soldiers await us there,' Imogen said. 'What can we do?'

I felt myself flush as Thomas looked deep into Imogen's eyes and said, 'Quick put your arms around me.'

'So what's the plan?' Imogen asked breathlessly.

'The plan is this,' Thomas said.

For a moment I thought he was going to lean over and kiss her. I'm sure I saw her move slightly towards him. But Mr Bolli saved the day.

'Now the stage directions say to kiss, but you don't have to do this. You can just hug and say, "I love you, Princess Jasmine."'

Thomas carried on staring at his script. He'd gone pink. What did that mean? Was he relieved, or disappointed? Imogen nodded in a business-like way, being all professional.

On Wednesday I woke early and needed the loo. On the way back I opened the curtains and saw that Jack Frost had decorated my window during the night. He must have brought his Selecta pencils because the patterns were so pretty and complex. In a quarter of an hour, Cara was due to turn into York Road, the milk float humming gently and the little orange light on the top blinking softly. I shivered, my feet turning to ice on the cold wooden floor, and I hopped back into bed to keep warm.

I'd nearly gone back to sleep when I heard a clink down below. I sprang out of bed and put on my Ugg boots and thick dressing gown. Then I flew down three flights of stairs, through the dark sitting room to the window. It took a bit of effort to open it as frost had formed outside, but I managed it and scrambled out, leaping over the wall to the porch just as Cara came through our front gate, carrying two bottles of milk and one orange juice.

'Good morning, little miss,' she said. Cara has this clever way of talking in a normal voice whilst being quiet. The opposite of a stage whisper.

'Good morning, Cara,' I replied, trying and failing to do the same.

'Shh,' she said, handing me the orange juice, which I nearly dropped.

'Girl, you're going to catch your death,' she said, seeing what I was wearing. Then she made me go back into the house and get a thick coat.

I followed her down to the float and got in. She asked me how things were going at school and I told her about the play and how trying to be friends with Imogen hadn't gone quite as well as I'd hoped.

'I'm more worried about Emily though,' I said. 'We had a bit of a falling out.' I told her about the photos, and how I felt betrayed.

'It sounds like you were pretty hard on her,' Cara said as she got out of the float to make a delivery to Mr Campbell.

'SHE STARTED IT!' I cried, only for Cara to shush me. I waited till she came back before going on. 'She was laughing at a picture of me with make-up on.'

'Why did you have make-up on?'

I shrugged. 'For fun.'

'So why can't Emily join in the fun? I'm sure she wasn't doing it to be mean.'

'No, but she hurt my feelings,' I protested.

'And telling her how you felt was the right thing to do, but you shouldn't be too hard on her. It sounds like you took a silly picture, people laughed at it and you got cross.'

I hadn't thought about it like that. 'Well she put on make-up,' I pointed out, not wanting to give in entirely. 'And a dress!'

'So what? Why can't she?'

'Because it's Emily, she doesn't do that. She's not friends with Imogen. When I saw her in the street, all dressed up, it was like I didn't know who she was any more.'

Cara didn't say anything, she stopped the float but made no move to get out, she just listened to me as I went on.

'Emily scowls, and is sarcastic, and she doesn't care about anything,' I said.

'Maybe you don't know her as well as you think you do,' Cara said. 'Maybe there's more to Emily than you thought. Maybe she has feelings, underneath the scowl. And maybe you hurt those feelings.'

I shook my head. It felt like Cara was telling me off. I felt my face grow hot. This wasn't supposed to be how it was. Cara was supposed to be supportive and tell me

I was amazing. But by the time we'd gone down to the end of York Road, then back, I'd started to think that maybe she was right.

Usually Cara does the deliveries to the odd numbers, including number 37, where Emily lives. But this time I asked if I could do it. Cara grinned and handed the two bottles to me. I grabbed one of the little cards Cara uses to write messages to customers and scribbled a big SORRY and a picture of a cat. Then I folded it over, wrote 'Emily' on the outside and took the milk and note down the path to my friend's house.

As we left the house a couple of hours later, on our way to school, I noticed Emily sitting on the low wall at the front of her house. She saw us and stood, falling into step beside me as I walked down York Road.

'Soz,' I said, after a while.

'Don't woz,' she said.

Masterclass

After school I watched a Sophia Loren film that Mummy had recorded for me off the TV. It was an Italian film called *La Mortadella* and was brilliant, even though it was old and had subtitles. Sophia Loren plays an Italian woman who's trying to get a big leg of mortadella ham through an airport in New York and she ends up falling in love with the policeman who's trying to stop her. Sophia Loren is very beautiful and is a brilliant actor. Most of all though, you can tell she's very, very professional.

As I watched I heard a voice from behind me. 'Sophia!'

I turned to see the Unknown Builder peering through the window, watching the TV. He clearly adored Sophia Loren too.

He looked at me, smiled wistfully and said, 'Mystychz bszyara.' Or something like that.

'I know,' I said, turning back to the screen. 'Mystychz bszyara.'

Mummy swept into the kitchen after dinner in a cloud of perfume that made Daisy look up from the Zoella masterclass she was watching. Mummy could show Zoella a thing or two about make-up, I thought. She was wearing a very pretty dress, dark blue, with lace around the arms. I sometimes wish I could wear pretty clothes like Mummy but I don't think it's for me, really. I'm more of a jeans and a T-shirt sort of girl.

'You told me you were going out,' Mummy said to Jacob.

He was sitting at the kitchen table, texting furiously. I was sketching a sparrow and William D was messing about with his Pokémon figures in the hall. He got exactly zero stars this week. He had a play date at Zachary's house and disgraced himself by jumping up and down on Zachary's mummy's bed with muddy feet.

'I am going out,' Jacob said. 'But later. Daisy and Chloe want me to help them rehearse their play.'

Mummy's eyes widened. 'That's very noble of you.'

'Well, you know me,' Jacob said modestly.

'He's getting phone credit,' Daisy pointed out.

'You're charging for your theatrical services?' Mummy said.

'It's more a case of returning a favour,' Jacob said hastily.

'Well I'm glad to hear you are going out,' Mummy said. 'Otherwise we would have wasted all that money on the babysitter.'

Front Door chose that moment to sound doorbell, as though she'd been listening to Mummy.

191

'I'll get it, I'll get it,' William D screamed. Daisy sprinted too. William D was much closer but he was slowed down by the heavy bag he wore, overflowing with BattleMaster figures. We all craned our necks to watch the race.

'DAISY!' William D wailed as she overtook him.

But at the last minute she stopped and let him win.

'HA!' he said, rounding on her. 'Beat you, beat you. I'm the King of the Castle.'

'First the worst. Second the best,' Daisy countered.

'Loser!' William D said, making a backwards L sign on his forehead.

'Will you please open the flipping door?!' Mummy cried.

Daisy managed to get Front Door open while William D 'helped'. I watched Jacob's face as he saw who was standing there on the threshold.

'Charlie,' Daisy cried. 'How lovely to see you. You're just in time to help us rehearse for our school play.'

Jacob turned to look at me. He gave me a wry smile. I looked back innocently.

'Well played, Grand Vizier,' he said. 'Well played.'

192

The Kiss

'So, in this scene, Jasmine and Aladdin are trapped together in the cave which is flooding with water,' Daisy explained breathlessly.

'I don't remember this from the film,' Charlie said, scanning the script.

We were in the sitting room, which I thought was more likely to encourage canoodling than Daisy's room. Jacob wasn't paying attention, he was on his phone. I frowned at him. Charlie was due to leave for Kenya in a week. This was Jacob's last chance to win her back and what was he doing? Playing Subway Surfer.

'Aladdin realises that there's no escape. And that this is his last chance to declare his love for Princess Jasmine,' Daisy said slowly, looking over at Jacob meaningfully. 'He grabs her around the . . .'

'Which of you is playing Princess Jasmine?' Charlie asked, interrupting.

'You are,' I said.

'And who is Aladdin?'

'Jacob,' I said.

'What?' Jacob asked, looking up at the sound of his name.

'I see,' Charlie said. 'This is just a read-through, yes?'

'No, no,' Daisy said. 'You have to act out all of the stage directions. It's really important. To help us with our preparations.'

'And what's your part in the play?' Charlie asked her.

'I'm the prompt,' Daisy said.

'And yours?' Charlie asked me.

'The Grand Vizier.'

'You're not even in this scene,' she pointed out.

'Can we just get on?' Daisy asked impatiently.

'Yes,' Jacob added. 'Let's just get this over and done with.'

Charlie looked at him and raised an eyebrow. 'Fine,' she said. She stood and read from her script. 'The water is rising, Aladdin, there's nowhere to go.'

'Do you think you can swim back the way we came?' Jacob read, woodenly.

I rolled my eyes. Mr Bolli would be waving his arms around at this point.

'No, it's too far, and the Vizier's soldiers await us there,' Charlie said dramatically, draping an arm across her forehead.

Daisy nodded in appreciation.

'What can we do?'

Jacob swept back his hair and looked deep into Charlie's eyes. I grinned. Jacob is very handsome sometimes. But then he ruined it by reading out his line in a monotone.

'Quick put your arms around me.'

'No, no, no,' I said, unable to bear it. 'You have to put more life into it. Like this: *Quick, put your arrrrms around me.*'

Jacob shrugged. '*Quick, put your arrrrrrrrrrrrrrrms around meeeee.*'

Charlie frowned, but she took a step forward and loosely wrapped her arms around Jacob. He grinned at her. Their faces were now very close together. Charlie was trying not to smile. Daisy was hopping up and down in excitement.

'So what's the plan?' Charlie/Jasmine asked.

'The plan is this,' Jacob/Aladdin said, leaning in to kiss her.

Daisy clenched her fists in anticipation. My heart leapt into my mouth. This was actually going to work!

But Charlie broke away. 'Jasmine's wet,' she said.

'Of course she's wet, they're in a flooded cave,' I pointed out. What was she doing?!

'No, I mean she's all pathetic,' Charlie said. '"I *can't* swim so far, *hold* me, Aladdin." I think the real Jasmine would be more kickass. She'd slap Aladdin, swim back down the passage and karate chop all the soldiers.'

'It's just a play,' I said.

'Yeah, it's just a play,' Jacob said, trying to hug her again.

195

'Get off,' she said and pretended to punch him.

Jacob pretended he'd been hit and fell back. He pulled out an imaginary pistol and fired at Charlie who dived out of the way. William D came running in at that point and launched himself at Charlie as she tried to stand up. She shrieked and tickled him until he squealed. So that was the end of the rehearsal, we played gun battles around the house for the next half an hour until Jacob remembered he was supposed to be going out.

'I'll text you,' he said to Charlie as he was leaving.

'Whatever,' Charlie replied casually.

We had mixed feeling about how things had gone. I said I thought it had mostly worked out how we wanted, even if they didn't actually go ahead with the kiss. Daisy disagreed.

'If they can't even do a stage kiss, then they're never going to do a proper one,' she said.

But I remembered what Imogen had told me, about being professional. 'I think the fact that they didn't want to kiss is a good sign,' I said, tapping my nose. 'If they can't be professional, it's because they're taking it personally.'

'That doesn't make any sense,' Daisy said.

'Trust me, Daisy,' I said.

Go Team!

Mr Peterson is looking increasingly mournful. When I got home after school on Tuesday, I found Piotr giving him a pep talk in the kitchen. Ana stood behind him rubbing his shoulders.

'We do this together, yes?' Piotr said, patting Mr Peterson's hand. 'This house will not beat us. Never!'

Mr Peterson nodded. It turned out they'd discovered more rising damp in the spare room which would need to be tackled before they could rebuild the wall over Front Door. The builders have quickly become part of the furniture. In a way, I don't want them to ever finish the house. I like them being here when I get home after school, and they try to make sure they've got all the serious hammering out of the way by then. William D loves Mr Peterson and follows him all around the house handing him tools and offering advice. Daisy is teaching Ana how to speak English and reading her bits from the Aladdin script. Ana can now say 'Curse the Vizier!' and 'Quick! Hide in here.' Which is real progress.

Mummy is no closer to deciding on a colour for the

sitting room. She texted Daddy and asked him to bring back some German tester pots in case colours there are any different. Mr Peterson keeps reminding her they'll need to order it soon and Mummy gets a panicked look on her face.

That night Mummy was super-busy with us all. She's always busy but when Daddy's not here she's even busier than ever. He might not seem to do a lot when he is here, but at least Mummy can get him to stir a pot or answer a phone while she gets on with something else. Tonight she was putting cream on a scratch I got from The Slug, helping Daisy with her homework, resetting the broadband, phoning Jacob to find out where he was. 'Family Admin' she calls it. Currently she was sitting at the table with William D, a book of bible stories open in front of her.

Mrs Duvall has told Mummy she needs to help William D with his religious studies. The infant school is a church school but we don't really go to church very often. Just at Christmas. So William D struggles a bit with R.E.

Mummy was quizzing him for a change. 'Where did Jesus and his disciples stay the night before he was crucified?'

'The garden centre,' William D said confidently.

'The Garden of Gethsemane,' Mummy corrected. 'OK, what did the Good Samaritan do?'

William D thought for a bit. 'Taxi driver?' he guessed.

'Not his job! What did he do in the bible?'

'I don't know,' William D replied.

'He helped a traveller who was lying by the side of the road,' Mummy explained.

'What? Helped him into the taxi?' William D said.

'Never mind,' Mummy sighed. 'How did Jesus feed the multitudes?'

'A pizza?' William D guessed.

'There were five thousand people!'

'I know, I meant All-You-Can-Eat.'

Mummy slumped on the table. 'You'll never get to play Joseph if you don't learn this stuff.'

We were interrupted by Clematis, who came in carrying something dead and dropped it next to the food bowl. I rushed over and picked it up with some kitchen roll. It was a type of mouse with a long nose.

'Oh, that's revolting,' Mummy said.

'It's a mouselet,' William D said. He can never remember the names of baby animals. He calls piglets piglings and baby swans singlets. 'Why does Clematis kill things?' he asked, coming over to peer at the little creature.

'Cats are hunters. It's in their nature,' I said. 'Everything eats something. Insects eat plants, birds eat insects, cats eat birds. It's Nature's Law.'

'The Circle of Life,' Mummy said.

'Hakuna Matata,' William D added. 'Which cat is this?'

That's another odd thing about William D, he can't tell the cats apart. Both cats are browny-black, it's true, but Clematis is thinner, has bigger eyes and moves around a lot. The Slug is fat and fluffy and just sits there with slug goo around his mouth.

'This is Clematis. He's brought the mouse in to offer it to us,' I explained. 'He's grateful for the food we give him, so he's contributing to the family's food. They're very sociable animals, cats. You have to thank them for the food they bring. If you get cross at them they think they haven't brought the right thing and go off and get something flappier.'

'Maybe he could get us a bigger turkey,' Mummy suggested.

'Thank you, Clematis,' I said carefully.

'Thank you, Clematis,' William D repeated, stroking him. Clematis purred and rubbed his cheek against William D's fingers. 'But I don't really want to eat that little mouse.'

I took a photo, then wrapped the poor little thing up and took it out to the bins. Dinner was ready when I got back, but William D wasn't eating. Mummy pointed meaningfully at his star chart, still mostly empty. He sighed.

'Just try it, William D,' Mummy said, standing over him. 'I'm sure you'll like it if you try it.'

William D screwed up his face, held his nose, closed his eyes and put a tiny morsel of chicken into his mouth.

Then he opened his eyes, looked up at Mummy and nodded. We all breathed a sigh of relief.

'That's what I like to see,' Mummy said. 'Children who like to try things. Not drugs though,' she added, walking over to the sink.

Since we couldn't afford the dishwasher tablets the other day, we're washing up everything by hand. Daisy and I have been doing the dinner plates.

'This food is delicious,' Daisy said. 'Thank you, Mummy.'

'Yes, thank you, Mummy,' I added. 'I really like the meat.'

'It's a little tough,' William D said. 'Slightly overdone. And the sauce is heavy on the tarragon.'

'Right, that's it,' Mummy said, pointing a soapy spatula at him. 'No more MasterChef for you.'

She turned back to the sink, then spun round again. 'I didn't even put any tarragon in!'

'Next time you should,' William D said and Mummy laughed.

She finds it hard to stay cross with William D. She says he's the funniest human on the planet. William D knows she thinks he's funny and always plays the clown to get out of trouble. He's a lot like Daddy, I think. I wondered where Daddy was just then, and whether he was laughing as much as the rest of us.

Today William D. smuggled a screwdriver into the school and attempted to disassemble the playhouse during break. He says the playhouse has a damp problem and needs fixing. We had a talk about this and he showed me some other items he'd brought in, including a hammer, some rawl plugs and a spirit level.

It's great to see William D working hard on his fine motor skills but it might be best if he was discouraged from doing this at school with a 2lb claw-hammer.

S. Duvall

Sweet Sorrow

<u>Goodbye Charlie</u>
A short play by Chloe Deal

Int: Kitchen. Early evening. Lights are low. Onstage are Mummy, Chloe, Daisy, William D. Jacob is offstage. Pleasant, cheerful incidental music.

SFX: There is a knock at Front Door.

Daisy and William D rush to answer but are unable to open Front Door. Mummy walks across stage to assist.

Charlie enters Front Door.

Mummy: (surprised) Hello Charlie. How nice to see you.

Children: (chorus) Charlie!

Charlie: Hi Polly, hi guys. I just thought I'd pop in on my way home and say goodbye. I'm off to Africa tomorrow.

Music: Dramatic chord.

Children look sad. William D falls to stage, weeping.

Mummy: I think it's brilliant what you're doing. You're going to have an unforgettable experience. I travelled across Africa in my gap year. Such memories.

Chloe: Did you help street kids, Mummy?

Mummy (guiltily): Err . . . indirectly, perhaps.

Daisy: We'll miss you so much.

William D is still on floor, continuing to cry. This should be distracting for the audience. And actors.

Charlie: I'll be back by Christmas though, I think. There's a chance of my visit being extended.

Jacob enters, stage right, and stops in surprise at the sight of Charlie. Children and Polly watch exchange with interest.

Jacob: (stiffly) So you're off then?

Charlie: Yes. I'm off.

Jacob: Will you write?

Charlie: Can I not just text? They do have mobile phones in Africa.

Jacob: Fine.

Charlie: Fine.

Jacob: Bye.

Charlie: Bye.

Jacob exits stage right. Charlie exits stage left.

Curtain.

Murder!

Mummy phoned the school today to tell them she doesn't want to read William D's behaviour diary any more. 'Obviously if he hurts himself, or someone else, then please do get in touch,' she said. 'Otherwise, I don't really want to know.'

She saw me looking at her when she'd hung up. 'It sounds like they've got it all covered,' she said.

'But what about his star chart?' I asked. 'There are hardly any stars on it.'

Mummy sighed. 'When I signed up to the behaviour diary idea, I'd hoped there might be some examples of good behaviour, as well as naughty behaviour. But that hasn't happened. It's all naughty.'

'Did you think he might be better behaved at school than at home?' I asked.

'Hoped, rather than thought, but yes,' she replied.

There was another bird murder that day and Mummy was sweeping up feathers when I arrived home. She made me take the bird itself out to the bins. It was a huge woodpigeon.

'What happens if Clematis eats all the birds?' William D asked when I came back.

He'd clearly been worrying about this. I had worried about it too because there are a lot of cats in Britain, and if they all liked to hunt as much as Clematis did then surely the bird population of this country was in serious danger. So I had looked it up on the internet.

'Don't worry,' I assured him. 'Apparently birds are not in danger of becoming extinct in Britain because of cats. Cats usually only catch birds that are sickly or weak.'

'That woodpigeon didn't look sickly or weak,' Mummy pointed out as she rummaged through William D's schoolbag. 'It was huge.'

'Maybe it had a headache,' Daisy suggested.

'What's this?' Mummy said, pulling a note out of William D's bag.

'Uh-oh,' William D said as Mummy read it.

But it turned out to be good news. William D has been given a part in his school nativity, *It's a Baby!*

'You got a part, William D,' Mummy said, reaching for the star stickers.

William D now has six stars on his star chart. There are still great empty patches. He especially didn't get any stars last week because William P came over for a play date and they threw dozens of mouldy apples over the fence into Mr Coleman's garden and some of them landed in his fish pond.

Daisy and I got in trouble with Mummy for laughing when we heard about the apple incident. She said it is not a laughing matter and William D's behaviour is unacceptable but I could tell she thought it was quite funny too. This is often the problem with Mummy when William D is naughty. She can't help laughing and he gets away with it.

So anyway, time is running short and Mummy is looking for any excuse to give him a star now because apparently it's not enough to punish bad behaviour, you have to reward good behaviour. He got a star this morning for remembering to flush the toilet even though he took off his pyjama bottoms again and left them on the bathroom floor. My Observation is that Mummy is trying to think of any old thing to help William D get enough stars on his chart for the Playbox IV.

'Well done for getting a part, William D,' Daisy said supportively.

He shrugged. 'Everyone got a part. Even Zach.'

'What part does Zach have?' Mummy asked.

'He's a disabled sheep,' William D said.

Mummy frowned. 'It's good to see they're encouraging diversity,' she said, eventually. 'Why shouldn't animals with disabilities be included in the stable?'

'He has a line,' William D said.

'The disabled sheep has a line? What is it?'

'The king has come, he is gory.'

'Glory, possibly?' Mummy suggested.

William D shook his head. 'No, I think it's gory. *He is glory* doesn't make any sense.'

'No, I suppose it doesn't,' Mummy said.

'You know who is Joseph?' William D said, suddenly cross. 'Harry!'

'Harry will make a perfect Joseph,' Mummy said. 'He's quiet and well-behaved. Plus, his parents help out at the church most Sundays.'

'What part did you get, William D?' I asked.

But William D wouldn't tell me.

'He's a camel,' Mummy said. 'It's a good part.'

'A camel is NOT a good part!' William D shouted.

'Look, you get a song. Joseph doesn't get a song. He just stands behind Mary looking calm and forgiving.'

'How's the song go?' I asked.

But again William D refused to answer. Mummy sang it instead.

'I've got the hump, I've been walking all day.
I've got the hump and I have to say,
I've got the hump, I've got the hump,
I've got the hump on Christmas Day.'

'How do you know it?' William D asked her, suspiciously.

'I've had four children, William D,' she said. 'This isn't the first school nativity I've been to. I've seen *It's a Baby!* twice before. I've seen *No Room at the Inn* three

208

times. It's not bad, though the Archangel Gabriel's character is a little underdeveloped.'

'Have you ever seen *Aladdin*?' I asked.

'No,' she said. 'And I'm *really* looking forward to it.'

Was she being sarcastic? It's hard to tell with Mummy sometimes.

Windy-pops

On Wednesday, Emily, Tobias and I walked to Imogen's house after school for our weekly read-through. On the way Tobias was talking non-stop about football but he kept interrupting himself with big burps every minute or so.

'Slow down,' I told him. 'You're talking too fast.'

'Got to get the words out before the next burp,' he explained. He burped again. 'Windy-pops. Mum always says I eat too fast.'

Emily and I laughed. Tobias is so funny when you get to know him. Imogen didn't seem happy to see him though. She rolled her eyes but didn't say anything. She's still pretending to be nice but I think it's only a matter of time before she snaps and goes back to being horrid.

'Try not to burp so loudly while you're here,' I whispered to him. 'It's not polite.'

He nodded.

Imogen was really annoying at the read-through. Today she was giggling at everything Thomas said again, and this time I noticed she kept looking at me as she was doing it. I knew she was trying to make me jealous. I just ignored her and focused on my lines.

Ellen brought carrot sticks, pitta bread slices and hummus out to the summerhouse along with a big jug of squash, then she left us to it. We scoffed the food and got on with the rehearsal. It went pretty smoothly. Even Tobias just said his line without leaping on the floor. I could tell he was trying to keep his burps in because he kept making little swallowing noises.

Then we did the scene where I have my big speech. I go on about wanting to be Caliph, and marrying Jasmine, and imprisoning Aladdin. I'd worked really hard to memorise it all using the quite complicated mnemonic technique Mr Bolli taught me where each line is linked to an action or movement. So basically, rather than just saying the words, I had to move my arms and tap my feet as though I was on stage, walking around slamming my fist into my palm and stomping about in anger and so on. The gestures helped me remember my lines, but all through my speech I could sense Imogen watching me. I tried not to look back at her but about halfway through I did and saw she was smirking at my movements. Laughing at me.

Suddenly I felt very self-conscious and straight away I forgot my words. I froze. Everyone was silent. Then I had to look down at my script, find my place and start again. After that I just read the words, my confidence was gone and I could feel myself blushing. I rushed through to the end.

'Looks like you've got some work to do on that monologue,' Imogen said, her head to one side as though she was concerned and trying to help.

'You put me off,' I snapped. 'You were smirking at me.'

'I wasn't smirking,' Imogen said gently. 'I was smiling, encouraging you.'

'You were trying to put me off.'

'I'm sure Imogen wasn't trying to put you off,' Sophie said. 'You need to be able to block out the audience anyway.'

'Yes, block it out,' Imogen said.

'Thanks,' I said, trying to sound sarcastic.

'You're welcome,' Imogen replied. She turned to Thomas and touched his arm. 'Now where were we?'

'It's your line,' Thomas said.

'Oh yes, of course,' she said. 'Aladdin, what are we to do?'

I stopped listening. I know I shouldn't let her make me so cross. Sophia Loren wouldn't have got cross, but I couldn't help it. I sat there, grumpy, for the rest of the read-through. Towards the end, Jasmine has a monologue of her own. Of course Imogen knew it all off by heart, and she just said it fluently, looking at each of us in turn, confident as anything.

She'd just got to the bit where she expresses her

undying love for Aladdin when Tobias let rip the loudest, longest belch I have ever heard. It rattled the door of the summerhouse, it shook the glasses on the table, it nearly brought the house down, literally. When it was over we sat in stunned silence for a few seconds, before everyone burst out laughing.

The tension was broken in an instant as all the boys clapped Tobias on the back and he sat, looking delighted. Then I caught Imogen's eye, and of course she wasn't laughing. She was glaring at Tobias. And then she turned to glare at me too. We called it a day after that as it was getting late. But as we walked back across the grass, Imogen called me over.

'Don't bring Tobias again,' she said.

'What? Why not?'

'He's just too disruptive.'

'He's hilarious,' I said. 'He's going to be brilliant in the play.'

'This is my house,' Imogen said. 'You had no right to invite him in the first place. If you bring him again, then you're not welcome either.' Then she stormed off towards the orangery.

Mean Imogen was back.

We said goodbye to Tobias outside his house on Cromwell Street and carried on, talking about Imogen and what she'd said on the lawn, when we heard someone rushing up behind us. It was Tobias's mother.

213

'I just wanted to thank you for including Tobias in your rehearsals,' she said, puffing. 'I know he can be difficult, but he loves it. He talks about you all the time.'

'That's OK,' I said, feeling a bit embarrassed. I wanted to say why wouldn't we include him, but I knew what she meant. Tobias was hard work sometimes.

Emily stared at her shoes. I didn't have the heart to tell Tobias's mother that he wasn't invited any more.

'Anyway, thanks,' she said. 'And tell your mothers I said hi.'

'OK, Mrs Roper,' I said.

When she'd gone, Emily and I looked at each other, worried. Something would have to be done.

PART FIVE
December

Ruby Friday

I was a bit cross. Daddy had only been home about half an hour on Friday night when Mummy told us they were going out and we were having a babysitter. Charlie was in Africa helping street kids, so someone called Ruby was coming instead.

'How much is this Ruby charging?' Daddy asked as he put on a new shirt.

Daisy and I were in their room watching them get ready. Daisy was staring at Mummy intently as she put on make-up. I was stroking The Slug on the bed. He rolled onto his back and purred like a tractor. Clematis was on my lap, eyes half closed as I scratched his ears.

Mummy mumbled something in response to Daddy's question.

'What did you say? How much?'

'Fifteen pounds an hour,' Mummy said more clearly.

'How much?!'

'She's from a proper agency,' Mummy snapped back. 'With police checks and everything. She's trained in First Aid. She speaks Cantonese.'

'How much does one who only speaks English cost?'

Daddy asked. 'In fact she doesn't even need to speak English. And do we need the First Aid?'

'She's looking after your children!' Mummy pointed out. 'I read an article the other day saying each child will cost you around £250,000 over the first ten years. So what's another fifteen pounds?'

'Per *hour*,' Daddy reminded her. 'Fifteen pounds per *hour*.'

William D came charging in and leapt on the bed, scattering the cats.

'We're all in here now, are we?' Mummy said.

Anyway, when Ruby turned up, she was really nice and very professional. She played Bananagrams with us and let William D win. She asked us all about our schools and our friends. She'd asked Mummy when each of our bedtimes was. Mummy had had to think for a minute. Bedtimes are a bit random in our house.

'So William D needs to be in bed by eight p.m,' Mummy began.

Ruby looked surprised.

'I mean seven-thirty,' Mummy said quickly.

Ruby nodded.

'Daisy needs to go to bed by . . . err, eight-thirty?'

Ruby raised an eyebrow.

'No not eight-thirty,' Mummy said. 'Eight.'

Again Ruby nodded. Daisy looked horrified.

'And Chloe can go to bed at . . . nine?'

Ruby pursed her lips.

'Eight-thirty,' Mummy corrected herself.

Ruby smiled, satisfied. Mummy and Daddy hurried out of the house soon after. Ruby let us each stay up exactly ten minutes past the agreed bedtimes. It was like she'd read in the Book of Babysitting that you had to give the children a special treat like that to get them onside. She read a story to William D, made sure we all had water to drink and had brushed our teeth. So Ruby was nice. But I thought she seemed a little fake. Like she was just acting the part of being a good babysitter. She wasn't real, she wasn't a friend.

Most of all, she wasn't Charlie.

The Real Holly

The rule in our house, as laid down by William D himself, is that no one's allowed to talk about Christmas until his birthday is over. Of course we do talk about Christmas but we whisper when he's in the room. Well, the big day came and went. He had his party on Saturday. When you're six, you invite everybody to your party and everyone just runs around screaming and pushing each other over. The theme was Pirates and Princesses which is the easiest thing because all the boys have a Captain Jack Sparrow costume and all the girls have an Elsa costume. The only slightly sticky bit was when Holly Nielsen arrived with a big grin and thrust a present into William D's hands. He stared at her in horror.

'I didn't invite you,' he said.

'Hush, William D,' Mummy said as Holly's mummy blinked in surprise. 'You asked me to invite Holly.'

'Not THIS Holly,' William D said. 'I meant the other Holly. The REAL Holly.'

William D is a very rude little boy. To her credit, Holly N didn't seem bothered about whether William D had invited her or not. I grabbed Holly's hand and took her off to play with Daisy and some of the other girls. Daisy is very popular with little girls because she looks like a real princess and there were always three or four of them following her around staring at her eye-shadow and stroking her ponytail. Daddy dressed as a pirate and handed out amazing chocolate treats he'd brought back from Germany. I dressed as the Vizier, to help me get into practice. I was starting to panic a little about how soon the play was. I still wasn't sure I was going to remember all my lines, and as for catching that stupid snake, forget it.

The building work carried on outside on the scaffolding and in my attic room, but Mummy had banned the workers from coming into the rest of the house which made Mr Peterson look like he was going to cry.

Despite my worries, it was a pretty good party and the only slight disaster was when two of the Williams set off the fire extinguisher. The minute the last child had been given his party bag, Mummy slammed Front Door and turned around, looking exhausted.

'How many days till Christmas?' William D asked.

Saturday

The Saturday after William D's birthday was just the best day ever. We had pancakes for breakfast with some amazing chocolate spread Daddy had brought back from Germany. Then Mr Peterson turned up along with a huge truck and two men who put up scaffolding at the front of our house. We went and sat on Shouty Dad's garden wall opposite and watched them work. Mr Coleman came out to see what all the noise was about and rolled his eyes when he saw what was going on.

'I'm really sorry,' Mr Peterson explained, looking miserable. 'We need to repair the brickwork at the front, there's no other way.'

When it got too cold we came inside and Mummy asked us if we wanted to help decorate the trees. We have two trees in our house; one for the children and one for the sitting room. Mummy does the sitting-room tree on her own. She chooses a different colour scheme every year and makes up little bouquets of bells and ribbons which she hangs sparingly around the tree in a diamond pattern. She only puts one set of white lights on, never chooses the blinky setting and squints to make sure there aren't gaps.

Her tree does look quite nice I suppose. It's *tasteful*, like a tree in the window of John Lewis, but I think our tree is much better. We just put EVERYTHING on it. Tinsel, baubles, bells, old craft models of Santa that we made in infant school years ago out of toilet rolls. We add mouldy robins with the legs missing, chocolate money in bags, a twisted star at the top and string after string of multi-coloured lights all set to random. The cats always help and like to climb up inside and whack the baubles around until they shatter.

'How about we put our tree in the sitting room this year,' I suggested to Mummy when we were finished. 'You can put yours in the playroom?'

She came in to look at our tree. Clematis was about halfway up, his big green eyes looking out at us. The Slug was underneath, chewing on a robin.

'I don't think so,' Mummy said. 'Good work though.'

There were still loads of unused decorations in the box Mummy had brought down from the loft. There was just nowhere to put them on the tree.

'Can we put the other decorations up around the house?' I asked.

But Mummy shook her head. 'Not with all the work being done,' she said. 'The workers need bare walls so they can paint.' I was a bit disappointed, but at least we had our tree. I wrapped another long bit of tinsel around it just to be on the safe side and put the box away.

After lunch we went out into the garden and played a marathon games session including One-Eyed Stephen, Canoe Wars and Skink Hunt which now featured a new rule that all the Phase warnings had to be issued in German. William D struggled with 'gesundheit!' but loved saying 'achtung!'

We had pizza for dinner and then played Murder in the Dark until way past our bedtime, so we were all still up when Front Door opened and in walked Jacob with Taffeta, whose hair was messier than ever. William D had gone through tiredness and out the other side by then. He was completely wired and had staring eyes and a white face. Mummy and Daddy were in the playroom. Mummy was watching a film and Daddy was snoring lightly on the sofa next to her. She kept calling out 'bedtime!' but until she gets up and really shouts you don't have to pay attention. I think she liked that all the family was together again, and she wanted to stretch the moment.

Taffeta's eyes rolled when she saw we were still up.

'Make them go to bed,' Mummy called from the playroom when she saw Jacob. 'Oh, hello, Tabitha.' But she still didn't get up.

Jacob came into the kitchen and said he'd make everyone cheese on toast but then 'BEDTIME' and we all nodded as if we were going to do what he said.

'Would you rather be a forwards T. rex,' William D asked Taffeta, 'or a backwards Dalek?'

'What?' she asked, confused. 'I don't know what you mean.'

'Never mind, never mind,' William D said. He was looking slightly manic now. He really needed to get to bed. 'Would you rather be a blue boy, or a two-headed girl?'

'Why do I have to choose?' she asked frowning. 'Jacob?'

I shook my head. Taffeta just didn't get children. Not like Charlie. Admittedly William D wasn't making it easy for her, but still. 'You're home early,' I said, changing the subject. 'I thought teenagers stayed out all night.'

'When I'm a teenager I'm going to stay out all night,' Daisy said.

Taffeta sighed. She was leaning against the cupboards. I could tell she didn't want to be here.

'Just popped home to change my shirt,' Jacob said slapping down a plate of cheesy toast, smothered in ketchup. Jacob's the best at cheese on toast, we all grabbed a slice and blew on it madly to cool it down. 'We're going to a party in Guildford.'

'What's wrong with that shirt?' I asked. He was wearing a T-shirt and it looked clean to me.

Daisy snorted. 'He can't wear that to a party.'

William D leaned across to me and spoke in a stage

whisper. 'I think Taffeta should brush her hair before she goes to a party.'

'Shush, William D!' I cried, mortified. 'She looks lovely!' Even though she didn't and I sort of agreed with William D.

'Can we go?' Taffeta said to Jacob. But William D had taken a mouthful of cheese that was too hot for him so he stood on his chair, mouth open, squawking and pointing. Jacob leaned over and blew on the hot cheese in his mouth to cool it down. Taffeta's eyes bulged.

'Thanks,' William D said, mouth full and chewing.

Daisy and I giggled. But then disaster struck. William D tried to sit down, but he was so tired he slipped and fell right off and went down in a clatter of arms, legs and chair. The cheesy toast slice in his hand flew across the room and slapped into Taffeta, leaving a cheesy, greasy ketchup smear across the front of her dress.

Taffeta screamed. 'You stupid little boy!'

There was silence. William D blinked at her. Taffeta grabbed some kitchen roll and started dabbing at herself.

Then Jacob said, 'Don't speak to him like that.'

Taffeta spun and glared at Jacob. 'Look what he did! Why are these little . . . things up anyway?'

'This is our house, and this is my family,' Jacob said. He pointed down the hall. 'And that, over there, is our Front Door. And if you don't like my family then you can walk through Front Door and never come back.'

Taffeta narrowed her eyes, grabbed her handbag and stormed down the hall.

'Bye, Tabitha!' Mummy called from the playroom as she passed.

Front Door opened easily for once, apparently as anxious as the rest of us to be rid of the horrible Taffeta. She slammed it hard and Daisy and I exchanged a grin.

'Wow!' I said. 'That was quite . . . wow.'

'No one talks to my family like that,' Jacob said firmly. 'Now c'mon my little BattleMaster, you're going to bed.'

He lifted William D, slung him over his shoulder and carried him down the hall and up the stairs.

William D grabbed another slice of cheesy toast as they went past the table. 'Does cheese come from A) The Sea B) Trees or C) Outer Space?' he asked as they went up the stairs.

'C) Outer Space,' Jacob replied.

'Correct!' William D said and took a big bite.

Jacob gets children.

Stage Whispers

On Sunday I wanted to sleep in because we'd had such a late night, but I was woken by a tapping on my window at eight-thirty a.m. I got out of bed and put on my warm slippers before shuffling over to the window and opening the curtains. Tamsin grinned back at me, looking absolutely delighted. I blinked in confusion before remembering the scaffolding. I opened the window and helped her inside, feeling a bit like Wendy in Peter Pan. There was a reason Tamsin had arrived so early on a Sunday.

'I really don't think you're supposed to be climbing on there,' I said. 'Mr Peterson told us to stay off it.'

'Couldn't help myself,' Tamsin said.

I poked my head out of the window to see Tamsin's mummy looking up anxiously.

'What is she like?' Tamsin's mummy called.

I shrugged.

Tamsin went to wake Daisy while I went downstairs to let Tamsin's mummy in.

'Are we early?' she asked as I put the kettle on to boil.

228

'No, we're late,' Mummy said as she came in, yawning. 'It was a late night for the whole family.'

Front Door rang soon after and I opened it to see Emily standing there. She was scowling, but I knew now that her scowls didn't mean anything. Standing next to her was Tobias, looking really excited. Tobias's mother stood behind.

'Thank you so much for this, girls,' she said.

'That's OK,' I said. 'We couldn't really do it without Tobias.'

'Come in,' I said to Tobias. 'Tamsin's already here.'

After Imogen had banned Tobias from attending rehearsals at her house, Emily and I had decided that we should hold our own Super-Rehearsal. An all-day event. And that Tobias should be there too.

We decided there was no hurry. It was a sunny day and after breakfast we played BOOMball in the garden for a while. Then we squeezed through the Thicket to the summerhouse and read through the whole script. Tobias got a bit bored and went off to run round the garden from time to time but that was OK. It took quite a long time because people kept forgetting where they were and Tamsin had to play some of the parts and didn't know the play at all. She had a torch which she was using to shine on us at the times when she'd be shining a spotlight on us in the play itself.

Mummy made us all lunch. After that we ran through a few of the most important scenes in Daisy's room.

William D joined in. We decided to do the scene that Emily has her line in. Tamsin was shining torches on us from various angles from the top bunk of Daisy's bed.

'I wish I could get higher,' she kept saying.

In Emily's scene, as we were calling it, Aladdin (played by William D) and Jasmine (Daisy) are running away from the Vizier. Emily, playing the Friendly Merchant, says, 'Quick, hide in here!' and helps them into a big stone vase.

Then the Vizier's men (Tobias) come rushing in and start searching for them while I stalk about the stage rubbing my hands evilly, outlining my plan to marry the Princess and rule the kingdom. The audience boo at that point, or at least they're supposed to. I was actually a bit worried that they wouldn't boo enough. In this case, booing was good, like at the panto. This is the bit where Aladdin throws a snake at me and I'm supposed to catch it. I thought I should probably do a bit of practice with that. William D was playing Aladdin which wasn't going well because he insisted on carrying a sword and kept attacking me with it.

'You're the baddie,' he explained, whacking me on the bum.

Tobias laughed.

'It's a play,' I said. 'You've got to follow the stage directions.'

'That's stupid,' William D said. 'If this was BattleMaster, Aladdin would just cut the visitor in twain.'

'Vizier,' I said. 'Not visitor. Do you want to be involved in this or not?'

So eventually we got him to do it properly, sort of, and he and Daisy came rushing into the room.

'Quick, hide in HERE!' Emily screeched.

Daisy and William D leapt into the dressing up basket.

'You're saying it too loud,' I told Emily. 'You're supposed to say it in a stage whisper.'

'What's a stage whisper?' asked William D from the basket.

'It's where you say something loudly so the audience can hear, but you do it in a whispery voice so they understand the character is saying it quietly,' I said.

'Whatever,' Emily shrugged.

So I started my bit, where I walk about cackling and grinning.

'Soon Aladdin will be locked in the deepest dungeon, and the Princess will be mine,' I said. Then I did a deep, booming Bwouhahaha laugh. 'You're supposed to boo and hiss at me,' I pointed out to the others as they watched.

'Actually, you're really good,' Tamsin said shining a torch right into my face.

'Thanks,' I said, blinking. 'But that means you're supposed to boo even louder.'

'I'll never understand theatre,' Tamsin replied.

'William D, you have a line now,' Daisy said. 'One of the guards sneezes, and you say "Bless you".'

Emily was playing a guard now that her one line was done. She sneezed.

'Bless you,' William D said.

Emily whipped the top off the basket. William D gave her the thumbs up.

'No, you're supposed to throw the snake at the Vizier now,' Emily said.

William D reached down, grabbed the rubber snake and hurled it at me as hard as he could, hitting me in the face. So that still needs a bit of work. But there was no time to try again because just then Tamsin leaned a bit too far over with a torch and fell off the top bunk into a box full of Polly Pocket accessories. Tobias booed. She got a little cut on her arm and we all trooped downstairs so Mummy could put a plaster on it.

'Where's Ruby when you need her?' Mummy asked, looking for the First Aid box.

After that we had some cake and went outside to play Skink Hunt. Daddy joined in and it was totally brilliant because he introduced a new rule about being able to transmogrify during the second Thunder Phase which made it a LOT more fun. It turned out Tobias was brilliant at Skink Hunt even though he'd never played before. He's not really a great rule-follower, Tobias, but since the rules of Skink Hunt are quite changeable it doesn't really matter.

But when it started to get dark and it was time to come in, and for Tobias and Tamsin and Emily to go home, I got a bit sad. Daddy went into the playroom to start collecting his spreadsheets so he'd be ready to go first thing in the morning.

Christmas seemed a long way away.

A Tragedy

No Room at the Attic

A short play by Chloe Deal

Int: Kitchen. Sunday Evening. Onstage are Chloe, Daisy, Mummy, William D eating at table. Mummy is picking at William D's leftover food and drinking a glass of wine.

Chloe: December seems to be taking for ever.

Daisy: I know, I just want Christmas to hurry up and arrive.

Chloe: We have the plays to get through first. (They look at each other anxiously.)

Mr Peterson enters stage right, wringing his hands.

Mr Peterson: (dramatically) We've hit a little snag.

All: What is it?

Mr Peterson: I've been lying awake all night. I just can't see how we're going to get it finished before Christmas.

Mummy: You HAVE to get it finished by Christmas. In fact, by the 23rd. The Cooper-Deals arrive Christmas Eve. They need somewhere to sleep.

William D: They could sleep in the stable?

Mr Peterson: (despairingly) But we've discovered some of the joists have rotted. We have to replace those before we can lay the damp proofing which we need to do before we repair the wall over the front door. Only then can we get on with the decorating.

Mummy: (glaring) You told me you could finish the job by Christmas, and you'll just have to find a way.

William D: Follow the Yonder Star?

Mr Peterson: And another thing. We've had to do quite a bit of rewiring, and some of the wires need to go up into the loft.

Mummy: So?

Mr Peterson: You have bats. They have a protection order on them.

Mummy: We know.

Mr Peterson: So I can't disturb them by knocking holes in the walls. They're hibernating at the moment.

Mummy: (sighs) Honestly, we can't disturb

them when they're rearing their young, we can't disturb them when they're asleep. I wish someone would put a protection order on me so I could get some peace and quiet. Does this mean you can't finish until they wake up?

Mr Peterson: It means we have to send the wires through the attic room instead.

Chloe: You mean MY room?

Mr Peterson: Yep. It'll be messy I'm afraid, you'll need to move out.

Mummy: (smiling) Well that's probably for the best, it's about time Chloe moved into her proper room. Any chance we could paint over the Megadeath mural first though?

Mr Peterson: (Pulls face and shakes head.)

Mummy: We'll just have to leave the mural for now. I'll start moving Chloe's things tonight.

SFX: *Dramatic chord.*

Chloe: (to camera) Oh NO!

On the First Day of Christmas

That night I lay in my new bed, in my new room, completely unable to sleep. It was too hot for a start, and the moonlight peeped between the curtains and reflected off the skulls of the skellington band on the Megadeath mural. So that didn't help. The noises were all wrong too, the creaks and groans came from the wrong directions and sounded creepy instead of friendly. Our House was playing a different tune. I don't like it when things change. Why couldn't I stay in my little room for ever? Why couldn't the house be just like it was before? We didn't need new wallpaper, or new radiators, or lights that worked. I wanted things back to how they were, and I wanted Daddy back too.

The worst thing of all was that now I was at the back of the house, I wouldn't be able to hear the clink of milk bottles when Cara came by on Wednesday morning.

I don't think I got a bit of sleep and was yawning when Mummy called us all into the kitchen in the morning before school. Daddy was in Eindhoven of course, but the rest of the family was there. Daisy and me, William D, Jacob, Mr Peterson.

'Right,' Mummy said. 'There's one week until Christmas and it's the busiest week there has ever been in the whole history of weeks. It's going to be tough but if we all concentrate on what we have to accomplish we can do it.'

We all nodded.

'Tonight is the dress rehearsal for *Aladdin*,' Mummy went on. 'I have to collect William D from William P's house, so Jacob will collect Chloe and Daisy after school and you can walk back down to school with Vicky and Emily for the rehearsal in the evening. Tomorrow is the first performance. I can't go to that but William D will be watching. Jacob will take you to that. Wednesday is the second performance, I'm hoping I can come to that, if not, Jacob will take you again. Thursday is going to be busy. But I'll definitely be there if I'm not able to go on Wednesday. Vicky will collect you from school and walk you down to St Andrew's church. At four p.m, William D is having a dress rehearsal for his Nativity.'

'What?' William D asked.

'Your Nativity play,' Mummy said. 'Where you dress as a camel?'

'Is that still happening?'

'Yes, of course. In front of all the parents.'

William D shrugged. 'OK,' he said. He really doesn't pay attention.

'After that, Vicky will take you back to her house for your tea. I'll meet you there and take you back to your school for the final performance.'

'Yay!' I said.

'On Friday,' Mummy went on, 'William D has his Nativity play. Mr Peterson will have finished by then, isn't that right, Mr Peterson?'

Mr Peterson looked pale, but he nodded. 'As long as it doesn't snow,' he said.

'And the Cooper-Deals arrive on Sunday,' Mummy said. 'It'll be a tough week, but once it's over, it'll be Christmas. The perfect Christmas. And even though we'll be busy, we'll have fun too. Let's enjoy ourselves!'

'Hurrah!' Daisy said.

I nodded and smiled, even though I was feeling really nervous about *Aladdin* and the week ahead. Still, Mummy was right. One more week and it would be Christmas. Daddy would be back and the house would be finished. Jacob gave Mummy the thumbs up and William got up to do his Mexican Dance. The only one who didn't look happy was Mr Peterson, who was looking out of the window at a big black cloud that was sweeping towards us.

A Bad Dress Rehearsal Means a Good First Night

So that evening we were having a full dress rehearsal. Starting at 6.30 to give us time to go home and have something to eat first.

'Get some rest,' Madame Adams said. 'You're going to be tired. Eat, rest, have a nap if you can and we'll see you back at six-fifteen sharp.'

But it didn't quite work out that way for us. It started raining just as we left school and we were drenched by the time we got home. We ran upstairs to get changed. Luckily, William D was at a play date at William P's. The builders were upstairs, banging away as usual. I made a sandwich for Daisy and myself.

'Do we have to walk down to the school on our own?' I asked when Mummy had finished her phone call.

'You'll have to walk down with Vicky and Emily,' Mummy said. 'I need to go and collect William D. The Pearsons live miles away.'

'But it's raining,' Daisy pointed out. 'Our costumes will get wet.'

Mummy rolled her eyes. 'OK, you can come with me to collect William D, and I'll drop you off on the way back.'

One Hour Later

'I'm going to be LATE!' I shouted. My blood was boiling despite how freezing the air was. The rain had stopped almost, but tiny daggers of sleety rain still pricked at my face and hands.

Mummy inspected the jack carefully. 'Which way up does this go?' she asked.

We were on a quiet country road, about a mile from the school. It was pitch black, there were no other cars about and we had a flat tyre.

'MUMMY!' I cried. 'I can't be late. I just can't be. They can't start without me.'

'It's only a dress rehearsal,' Mummy said as she tried to position the jack under the car. 'They'll muddle through.'

'I'm one of the leads,' I said.

'You have an understudy,' Mummy said.

'It's OLIVER!' I shouted. 'Oh, you don't understand.'

She dropped the jack and stood to face me, suddenly cross. 'No, Chloe. YOU don't understand. I have a house full of builders, my husband is in another country. I have four children to look after and I face the imminent arrival of your father's insane relatives. I have a murderous cat, a missing teenager and a useless boss to deal with. And now I have a flat tyre. So if you can just calm down for a minute then maybe I can deal with that first, then we'll face some of our other problems. OK?'

We stood, glaring at each other for a while until we heard a car slow down and a voice said, 'Need some help?'

It was Toby, Imogen's dad, in an expensive-looking car. He pulled over and got out. 'I always stop for a pretty lady in need of help,' he said with a grin.

Mummy tried to smile back. 'Thank you,' she said. 'But I've got it covered.'

'I insist,' Toby said, rolling up his sleeves. 'I'm a whizz with tyres.'

While he fixed the tyre, I changed into my costume in the back of the car while William D ran a quiz for Daisy. Eight minutes later we were racing towards the school. It was now 6.27. I was definitely going to be late. As soon as Imogen's daddy had finished, Mummy had started the car.

'Thanks so much!' she'd said. 'I'm so sorry but I must rush.'

'See you around,' he'd said, looking a bit disappointed.

Mummy pulled up outside the school at 6.34 p.m. and I leapt out and raced down the path, leaving the door wide open. I arrived in the hall puffing and panting. Mr Bolli shook his head as I raced past and Madame Adams threw up her hands.

243

'This is not good, Chloe,' she said as I scrambled up the steps to see a relieved-looking Oliver scurry off the stage. Imogen stood there, looking disappointed.

'Not professional,' she said. 'Not professional at all.'

I got through the opening scene, where I have a couple of lines, then luckily I'm not on stage for a while. I stood in the wings, getting my breath back, trying the breathing techniques that Mr Bolli had shown me. Daisy trotted up, unconcerned about being late and sat in the wings with her script. A lot of the scenery was finished now and the lighting was being set up. I saw Tamsin walk past carrying a huge lamp like they have in fashion shoots. She tripped over the cable and I caught it just in time.

'Thanks,' she grinned. 'What am I like?'

'I think we need a single spotlight over there for the opening scene,' I heard Imogen saying to Mr Carter who was the stage manager. 'And then maybe all the lights should come on when I enter from the left. Or maybe just the stage lights to give a softer effect because . . .'

'You'll get what you're given,' Mr Carter said, before walking off.

The rehearsal didn't go very well. All the lines we'd memorised so carefully just seemed to drop out of our heads as soon as we were on stage. It was easy to do it in Imogen's summerhouse, or Daisy's room, but not here. Daisy had a lot of work to do, prompting people, which

I noticed she did without even referring to the script most times.

Everything took much longer than it was supposed to. When it was Tobias's turn he was nowhere to be found and someone said he'd just gone home. I saw Madame Adams in the back row shaking her head the whole time. Tamsin climbed up some scaffolding and had to be helped down by Mr Carter. All the time I was getting more and more nervous. I could remember my little lines. Daisy had done such a good job coaching me that I knew them all inside out and back to front. But there was the big speech to do.

I tried to keep my mind on other things and looked at the backdrops. Someone had drawn a huge crescent moon over the bazaar and had used a sort of creamy magnolia paint, a bit like the colour of the big tester-pot square in the sitting room next to the window. Below the Slight Cappuccino and next to the Button Mushroom. Under the stage lights though, it looked a little too yellowy, in my opinion – like there was a giant banana floating over Cairo.

'Chloe!' Daisy hissed, reminding me it was my cue.

I strode onto the stage and blurted out the first line. 'And now my time is near. Soon I will be Caliph and things will change . . .'

Slow down, Chloe, I told myself. I stopped, took a deep breath, then carried on more slowly.

'. . . Only two things stand in my way. The Old Caliph

himself, and that accursed Aladdin . . .' As I spoke, I trod purposefully, slapping my fist against my palm, remembering the cues and the signals. I felt my shoulders relax. I was nailing this. Maybe everyone else was forgetting their lines, but not Chloe Deal. Oh no . . .

. . . Oh no!

I had made the mistake of turning around and there, peeping out from under the lid of a great jar, was Imogen – watching me, smirking at me. And suddenly the words were gone. I forgot where I was supposed to be standing. I froze. The lights seemed so bright, the banana moon hovered over me, also staring. My mind was blank.

'. . . I must find some excuse to lock him away for ever . . .' Daisy hissed from the wings.

'I must find some excuse to lock him away for ever,' I went on. Thank heaven for Daisy! I struggled through the rest of the speech, keeping my back to Imogen throughout. But I was jerky and couldn't for the life of me remember the last line. I got to '. . . I must return to the palace now and make my preparations.' I knew there was a bit more to come but couldn't remember what.

'Prompt?' I whispered. 'Daisy?'

Daisy looked down at the script, puzzled. 'It's just a stage direction,' she said. 'The Vizier cackles.'

Of course! The cackle! How could I have forgotten that bit? I gave a half-hearted laugh, more like a cross between a chuckle and a cough, and stomped off stage, furious with Imogen, but even more furious with myself. Why had I ever thought I could do this?

First Night

I stood in the wings, a thousand tiny birds in my tummy. Mr Bolli stood next to me, his forehead glistening with sweat. He swallowed. He wasn't even going on stage and he was nervous. We could hear parents chatting out in the hall and the scrape of chairs as the late-comers found themselves seats. I peeked out through the curtains and saw William D sitting on the mat for the little ones at the front. He was with William H and Zach and all three were arguing about something. I looked further back and saw Imogen's mummy and daddy. Then just behind them were Tamsin's mummy and daddy, and Vicky Bellamy. Right at the back I saw Tamsin, who was standing next to a big spotlight. I looked for Mummy without thinking, then remembered she was at work. I hated the thought of her missing the first performance. Mr Bolli hauled me back as the lights went down in the hall and Tamsin shone her spotlight on to Madame Adams at the other side of the stage.

'Ladies and gentlemen,' she began. 'Welcome to the Weyford Junior School Christmas Pantomime. The children have all worked extremely hard to put on a great show for you tonight. I think you're going to be astounded. Now remember, this is a pantomime, so we want lots of cheers for the heroes, plenty of boos for the villain and don't forget to shout 'he's behind you!' at the appropriate moments. Now, without further ado, I give you . . . *Aladdin*!'

The curtain swept back, the stage lights came on. The play had begun! The opening bit was a song with all of the extras but not the lead characters. We stood together in the wings watching the show, hoping they'd get it right. A couple of people tripped up, Tarik was singing horribly out of tune and I think the words Jack was singing were from a completely different song. But they got through it OK and it was a lot better than the dress rehearsal.

'OK everyone,' Imogen said to our little group. 'Now, let's be professional out there tonight, let's nail this, but most of all, let's have fun!'

She's such a phoney, but I gave a fist pump along with everyone else. Then my heart sank a little as I watched Imogen turn to Thomas and give him a hug. She whispered something into his ear and he nodded and smiled.

As the dancers came off, it was time for Aladdin and the monkey to go out for the first scene. I watched for a while. Thomas was good – he had them all laughing as Sophie teased Aladdin, trying to steal peanuts off him. It seemed to be ages before they left stage right and it was Imogen's turn to come on. As she walked out there were more cheers even though she hadn't done anything yet. I rolled my eyes. Next to me, Emily scowled.

Eventually it was my turn to go on. I scrunched up my face, trying to look as evil as possible, adjusted my turban and strode onto stage. My heart was racing. I was met with complete silence. They were supposed to be booing, I thought. Why weren't they booing? I stood. Swallowing nervously, looking out into the darkness.

And then I heard William D, right at the front. He was on his feet, cupping his hands to his mouth and shouting.

'Boooooo. Booooo.'

'BOOOO!' everyone else suddenly cried.

Relief flooded through me. I'm not even sure William D realised it was me but he certainly knew what to do when a baddie appeared. I was grateful anyway. I waited for the boos to die a little, clapped my hands together and spoke my first line.

'Greetings, O Caliph,' I said greasily. 'How may I serve you today?'

From then on things ran pretty smoothly, barring a few incidents. Tamsin dropped a light and fell off a chair. Emily forgot to come on when she was supposed to, and Oliver, playing the palace guard role Daisy had vacated, forgot to leave the stage at one point and had to be dragged off. Daisy kept having to prompt him on where to stand. Tobias was a big hit though. He came sweeping onto the stage for his big entrance, circled the stage a couple of times and belly-flopped down like an aeroplane, sliding right across the stage and crashing into Oliver, knocking him over. This all got a great laugh even though it wasn't in the script.

One thing that did go wrong though was that I dropped the snake, even though Thomas came really close and gently threw it from a couple of feet away. It's supposed to be a big comic moment when I'm fighting with the snake before throwing it into the crowd, so it was a shame, but I was determined not to let it get to me.

Just before I was due to go on for my big speech, Imogen came up to me.

'Don't worry about dropping the snake, Chloe,' she said earnestly. 'Just concentrate on the speech.'

'Thanks for the advice,' I said, forcing a smile. 'By the way, your dress is on inside out.' Then I walked on stage, leaving her craning her neck to see. Another great BOOOO! rang out.

Stay calm, Chloe, I told myself. *Remember your physical reference points.* I held out my palms, waited for quiet in the audience, then began my speech. I stormed to one side of the stage. I stomped back to the other side. I reached high. I hunched my back. I clapped my hands and shook my fist. The words flowed. Not too fast, not too slow. The one thing I didn't do was look at Imogen. I didn't even think of her. I got all the way through my speech without making one mistake.

Almost.

Near the end, when I'm talking about all the horrible things I want to do to Aladdin, I heard a pop behind me and one of the stage lights went out. I turned, unable to help myself, and saw Tamsin rushing to a ladder, clearly intent on fixing the light. Madame Adams realised what she was doing and rushed to stop her, but you can't stop Tamsin climbing and up she went, quicker than Aladdin's monkey. A couple of seconds had passed and I realised I had to get back to my speech. I turned back and was just about to speak when I caught sight of Imogen in the wings. She winked at me.

I opened my mouth. 'I . . . I . . . the Caliph . . .' But it was no good, I'd let myself get distracted. The words had gone. I turned to Daisy, standing in the wings. Out of the corner of my eye I could see Tamsin dangling from a gantry just off stage and Madame Adams trying to rescue her, but I forced myself to look away. The last thing I needed was another distraction.

'The Princess will be mine. The Kingdom will be mine,' Daisy murmured, just loud enough for me to hear.

Then I was off again. I got through the rest of it without forgetting any more lines, but my heart wasn't quite in it. I left the stage to a few boos, but it seemed the audience's heart wasn't in it either.

We didn't get home till very late. The general feeling among the cast was that things hadn't gone very well. Vicky Bellamy dropped us home, where Mummy was waiting for us. The house was a mess – tools and torn bits of wallpaper all over the floor, dustsheets everywhere splattered with undercoat. It didn't look like our house, it didn't feel like home. But Mummy gave us a big smile and a hug.

'I'm so sorry I couldn't make it,' she said. 'How did it go?'

I shrugged. Daisy grimaced.

'It was really long,' replied William D.

'Those are tough first night reviews,' Mummy said.

'Will you definitely be there on Thursday night?' I asked.

'I definitely will,' she said.

'Family Deal?'

'Family Deal,' she said.

Festive Milk

I didn't really feel like getting up at 4.30 a.m. on Wednesday. I'd set my alarm, but when I woke the wind was shaking the house and wet snow was clattering against the window. I was actually quite glad of Sizewell B as it was so cold outside my room. But I needed some advice. And the best person for advice was already up and about. I was going to be tired tonight, but it had to be done. Only three more days, then I had two weeks of Christmas holidays to rest.

I pulled on some thick leggings and woollen socks, then I put on my dressing gown and went downstairs. The only light came from the frantic flickering of the multi-coloured Christmas tree lights visible through the open playroom door. Clematis trotted down the hall, miaowing quietly. I stopped to give him a hug before reaching up to the coat rack for my thick waterproof coat. As I opened Front Door, Clematis retreated, his tail fluffy like a bottle brush. The sleet stung my eyes and I was careful not to slip as I went down the steps.

I was early today and had to wait, hopping from foot to foot, until I saw the bright yellow light of the milk float turn into York Road. I ran up the street to greet Cara, who was wearing a Santa hat.

'What a morning for you to be up,' she said, shaking her head. 'Why aren't you tucked into your warm bed?'

'I haven't seen you for ages,' I said, climbing into my seat which was already warm, as if Cara had been expecting me. 'Plus I need some advice.'

'OK,' she said. 'But advice doesn't come free, you have to make some deliveries on the way.'

'OK,' I said with a grin.

And so Cara listened as I told her about all the things that were worrying me. About how Thomas liked Imogen, and how I was sure I was going to mess up my lines again tonight and how I missed Daddy and wanted him to be watching me in the play. Cara listened, then interrupted to tell me to deliver two pints of gold-top to the Fowlers. She also gave me a sprig of holly to stick between the bottles.

'Why?' I asked.

'Because it's Christmas,' Cara said. 'And I want to remind people that it's Christmas. Because Christmas is the perfect time to give a little bonus to your friendly neighbourhood milk lady.' She gave me an exaggerated wink. A stage wink, I suppose.

'How can I go on stage knowing that Imogen is just going to keep trying to put me off?' I asked when I got back to the float.

'What is it she's actually doing though, to put you off?' Cara asked.

'She . . . she . . . stands there watching me,' I replied. 'Smirking, laughing. Just being all . . . Imogen.'

'You have to be professional,' Cara said.

'You sound like her,' I told her.

'Well maybe Imogen is right this time,' she said. 'Look, a long time ago, when I first started delivering milk some people on my route wrote to the dairy and asked if they could have someone else delivering their milk.'

'Why?' I asked.

'Because they didn't want their milk bottles to be delivered by someone with dark skin,' Cara said.

I sat in shock for a moment. 'You mean they were racists?' I asked.

We learned about racism in school. But I wouldn't have dreamt anyone could be racist to Cara.

Cara shrugged. 'They were just ignorant. Mostly older people, with old ideas. You'd be surprised how many of them there are out there.' Then she got out to make a delivery, taking a gold-top, an orange juice and a sprig of holly.

'I'm sorry,' I said when she returned.

'You shouldn't be sorry,' Cara said. 'Most people don't even think of being racist, they don't see skin colour, but there are always a few.'

'So what happened?' I asked.

'Mr Nettleship from the dairy wrote back to them and said he wouldn't change my route, which made me cry a bit. Lovely man, Mr Nettleship,' Cara said and I think I saw her wipe away a tear.

'Did they cancel their milk order?' I asked. 'The racists?'

'One did,' Cara said, 'but the others kept up with it. I even got a little Christmas bonus from one of the families.'

'And you delivered milk to them? Even though they were racists?'

'Of course,' Cara said. 'I was professional. I did my job, regardless of everything else.' Cara stopped the float but didn't move to take an order. She looked me in the eye. 'Be professional, Chloe. Always get the job done, and don't worry about what other people say about you.'

As I said goodbye to Cara and walked back to our house, I saw a figure standing outside, looking up at the house in the golden streetlight. It was Piotr. He smiled when he saw me and I stood beside him and looked up at the scaffolding.

'Today is big day,' he said.

We were all tired and I'm not sure how I got through school. I had two more performances to do. What if I messed it up again at tonight's performance? I know Cara had said to be professional, but I was just so tired

I could hardly think. I couldn't concentrate on my school work and messed up my maths mock test. I hate trajectories.

I tried to rest when I got home. We had a couple of hours before we had to be back in the hall. But I couldn't sleep because Piotr was hammering somewhere in the house. Later Jacob walked me and Daisy down to the school. William D was at William H's house for a play date. We passed the level crossing and the row of shops near the station. When we got to the fish and chip shop, Daisy and I stopped and looked inside to where there was a big Charlie-shaped hole. We looked at each other sadly. Then I looked up at Jacob, who looked saddest of all. As we walked away I noticed that he checked his phone, then put it away.

'Have you had any texts from Charlie?' I asked.

He looked at me and nodded. 'She texted to say she's having a great time and she'll probably stay in Kenya until the New Year now.'

'Why don't you phone her?'

He thought about it for a moment, but then shook his head. 'I can't afford to phone Africa. Anyway it's not as if she's my girlfriend or anything.'

But I saw his face as he said this and I could tell he was really sad. I think Jacob was starting to realise what he was missing.

When we got to the school Mr Bolli saw me and

ushered me backstage. 'Tonight, Chloe. You are-a going to be amazing,' he said.

'Like Sophia Loren?' I asked.

'Exactly like Sophia Loren,' he agreed. 'You go out there and have fun!'

'Red leather, yellow leather, red leather, yellow leather,' Imogen was saying, enunciating carefully. Tobias was practising his slide across the floor. I caught Emily's eye and we grinned at each other. Suddenly I felt good about it all. There's something about the thrill of performing that takes over and gets you all excited inside. I WAS going to be amazing. I WAS going to have fun. Most of all, I was going to be professional.

It seemed to take ages for the show to start and I kept going over my lines and the accompanying movements. I couldn't let a mistake happen like it had last night. I wouldn't let Imogen win this time. After what seemed like an age, it was my turn to come on stage. I had to walk right past Imogen, who smirked at me. At least, I assume she smirked at me because I didn't actually look at her. I strode to the middle of the stage, turned to the audience and gave a great hiss.

I waited.

And waited. The boo wasn't going to come, just like yesterday. I was aware of Imogen standing in the wings, watching me fail. I cleared my throat and was about to say my first line when a loud, clear 'Booooo' came from the back of the room. It was Jacob. Another brother had come through for me.

'BOOOOO!' he cried louder. Then someone else joined in. 'Booooo! BOOOOO!'

And then the entire house erupted in booing. I waved my arms around pretending I wanted them to stop booing, they booed even louder and I loved it. I tried not to grin – it wouldn't be in character. When the boos had died a little, I spoke my first line. And suddenly everything seemed to click into place and before I knew it my opening scene was over. '. . . The Caliph comes,' I finished. 'I must away!'

As I strode off, I heard a roar of BOOOOs behind me. Mr Bolli grinned and gave me a big hug. I grinned back at him.

'They love-a you, Chloe,' he said. 'That's what all those boos mean. That they love-a you.'

And that's how it went on. I strode, I turned, I pointed. I hissed and cackled and shrieked with rage. I came off when I was supposed to. I went back on when I was supposed to. I didn't forget a word. And throughout it all I got boo after boo after boo.

I even caught the snake.

It seemed like no time at all before it was time for my big speech. But I wasn't even nervous. I rolled right through and it was over before I even realised. Mr Bolli gave me a big thumbs up as I came off, and I could hear Jacob right at the back, booing louder than anyone.

Unfortunately the play wasn't completely perfect and it was sort of Tobias's fault, I'm sorry to say. When it was his cue he came racing on to the stage, dived and slid right across the polished floor. I could see his grinning face as he came whizzing across at a terrific speed. Unfortunately he misjudged his trajectory, which isn't really like him, and clattered right into Imogen, who went over in a tangle of arms, legs and chiffon. She was furious and after she got to her feet she was so angry she forgot her lines. Good Chloe felt bad for her. Bad Chloe muttered, 'Serves her right.' I don't like Bad Chloe sometimes.

During the next song, when we were back in the wings, I walked up to her and told her she'd done really well but I think she thought I was being sarcastic and glared at me. Then she rounded on Tobias.

'What did you think you were doing?!' she hissed at him.

'Sorry,' Tobias said. 'It was an accident.'

But Imogen turned her back on him and looked at Thomas who had walked up. 'I knew they shouldn't have let him be in the play.'

'Why shouldn't he be in the play?' I asked.

'Because he's a . . .' And then she used a word that you shouldn't use.

Lots of us heard it. Hannah and Emily and Tamsin and me and Tobias himself. And Thomas. There was a long pause.

'Don't use that word,' I said to Imogen.

She just glared back at me. My eyes flicked over to Thomas's face. I could see his mouth pursed in a line and little red spots appeared on his cheeks. Was he cross at me for snapping at Imogen?

'Chloe's right,' he said to Imogen. 'Don't ever use that word again.'

Imogen stormed off in a huff. Thomas looked at me and I looked back at him . . .

And then my heart sank when I saw him turn and go after her. Why would he go after her after what she'd said to Tobias?

I was relieved and happy after the show had finished and we went back on for three curtain calls. I got loads of boos when I went for my bow but then they turned into cheers. After the third curtain call Imogen went up to Tobias and said sorry and I could see she was crying. Sophie and Hannah gave her hugs and I shook my head. Just because she'd apologised everything was OK and she was the victim now? Thomas stood by, watching all this. I turned to see Emily standing there watching as well. She looked at me and shrugged.

'Typical man,' Emily said.

I think she could see I was upset. I'm not the only one who's good at Observing.

She gave me a quick hug. 'You were really good,' she said.

'You were really good as well,' I said.

'Shut up, Chloe,' she said with a grin. 'I only had one line: "Quick, hide in here!"'

'Yeah, but the way you said it made me want to quickly hide in there.'

We laughed a bit and hugged again. But on the way home I couldn't stop thinking about Thomas running after Imogen. We stopped off at William H's to pick up William D. William H's mum came to the door. She looked as tired as I felt. It was late for the little ones to be up and William D can be even more tiresome than usual when it's late. As he rushed out of the house Jacob stopped him and said, 'What do you say to Mrs Harrison?'

William D looked up at her, his face screwed up in thought. 'Sorry?' he suggested.

When we got home Jacob took William D upstairs for his bath. I wanted to thank him for booing me so I made him a cup of tea and took it up to the bathroom. But as I approached I heard him inside, talking on his phone. I used my Observation skills to listen to his conversation. I hoped he wasn't talking to Taffeta.

'I made a mistake,' he said. 'Haven't you ever made a mistake?'

'. . .'

'I know, I'm an idiot. But I've learnt my lesson. It's you I want.'

My heart sank. He was talking to Taffeta. I knew he didn't have enough phone credit to be phoning Charlie in Africa and who else could it be? How could he be trying to make up with Taffeta after all she'd said?! He was even worse than Thomas.

'Please come back,' he said.

I took the cup of tea back downstairs and tipped it down the sink.

Emily was right about men.

Third Night

The house is in a real state. There's plaster dust everywhere, all the wallpaper is stripped off and a lot of the floorboards are up. The scaffolding is still up at the front and Mr Peterson says the bricks have been redone but they all look a different colour and the cement between them is dark and it doesn't look finished at all. Mr Peterson came to see Mummy as we ate breakfast.

'I need this house finished by the day after tomorrow,' she reminded him. 'The Cooper-Deals are here on Sunday.'

'Don't worry,' Mr Peterson said. 'I know it looks a mess, but it's all cosmetic. Lick of paint, nail down the boards, coat of varnish on the spindles and it'll look like a show home.'

Mummy nodded, satisfied, but behind Mr Peterson I could see Ana, who was frowning as he spoke. Either she was frowning because she was struggling to understand him, or because she could understand him very well and thought he was talking rubbish.

'And while we're on the subject of paint,' Mr Peterson added. 'It's time for you to make a decision on the colour for the hallway.'

'I'm not ready,' Mummy said, panicked.

'Would you like me to choose for you?' Mr Peterson said. 'I know my paints. I'm quite partial to Subtle Envelope. Or Seraphim Breeze.'

'Yes,' Mummy replied. 'No. I don't know.'

'You've got twenty-four hours to decide,' Mr Peterson said. 'Then I'm going to go ahead and buy seventy-five litres of Subtle Envelope.'

Imogen wasn't at school today. I expect she was 'resting' for her final performance. It was a strange day at school. We didn't do much actual school work. On the one hand we were tired and ready for the term to be over, on the other hand those of us in the play, which is most of the school, were really excited. Emily and I took a walk around the playground at lunchtime to try and settle our nerves. We just happened to pass the football field and I saw Thomas there playing in goal. He looked over and saw me looking but I turned away, I was still cross with him for running off after Imogen.

'He's looking at you,' Emily said, craning her neck.

'Just keep walking,' I said, not turning, even though I wanted to.

'Now he's waving.'

'Ignore him,' I said, quickening my pace.

'He's running over towards us.'

'Stop looking at him!' I said.

'Chloe,' Thomas panted as he reached us.

I turned and pretended to be surprised to see him.

'I was waving at you.'

'Oh, hello Thomas,' I said frostily. 'I didn't see you.' Behind him I saw the ball trickle into the goal, which was now empty of course. His team mates roared at Thomas in disapproval but he ignored them.

'I don't think Imogen's really resting,' he said. 'I think she feels really embarrassed about what she said.'

'Is that why you ran after her?' Emily asked. 'To give her a hug and make her feel better?'

'No,' Thomas said. 'I went after her to tell her she needed to apologise to Tobias.'

'Oh,' I said. 'I thought you liked her . . . I thought . . . you know.'

He pulled a face. 'No, she's awful!'

'So why did you write your name under hers on the audition list?' I asked.

He looked at me and blushed. Then he shrugged. 'I just wanted to be in the play,' he said.

'You really don't like Imogen?' Emily asked.

Thomas shook his head. 'She's just so fake. She's not real, like . . . other people.'

There was a long silence after that. I knew that when Thomas said 'other people' he meant me. My tummy felt funny and I wanted to jump up and down. But I actually acted totally cool about it. I watched the boys playing football. Oliver was in goal now.

'Anyway, I thought we could . . .' Thomas said,

eventually looking at me. 'I wondered if we should, you know. Practise?'

'If we don't know our lines by now then we never will,' I said.

'Not our lines,' he said. 'Your catching.' Then he reached into his pocket and pulled out a large rubber snake.

About Last Night

I came home after school hoping for a rest before our last performance only to find that the house was a hive of activity. The Unknown Builder was messing about on the scaffolding. Inside, Piotr was hammering boards down on the first floor landing, watched by a delighted William D. Ana was painting outside my room, but it looked like she'd just started. Mummy had finally decided on Morning Spinnaker, to everyone's relief. The other builders were varnishing the spindles on the staircase. The smell of the varnish made me feel a little sick and I went to my new room and shut the door. I tried to shut the noise and the smell out and practised my big speech for the thousandth time. My tummy churned and boiled with nerves. But I was used to it by then. I knew the nerves would go as soon as I heard that first boo.

Mummy was working late again, but she'd promised she'd be there at the final performance and I knew she wouldn't let me down. Mrs Bellamy came over around 4.15 p.m. and walked us down to the church where William D was having the rehearsal for his Nativity play. Then we were going to have a quick tea at her house before all heading back to school for the last performance. Mummy was going to meet us there. William D is still not happy about being a camel, but Mummy said he could have a big star on his star chart if he stopped moaning about it and that seems to have worked.

When we arrived, Daisy and I were delighted to find out that Shouty Dad was there and in charge of directing the performance.

'STOP CHEWING BABY JESUS,' he shouted at Mary, who was being played by Eliza Roberts.

Emily groaned when she saw Shouty Dad. 'Not him,' she said. 'He's always shouting.'

'We like Shouty Dad,' I said. 'Daisy and I often Observe his family's behaviour from my window.'

'It's all very well Observing from over the road,' Emily replied. 'But you don't have to live next door to him.'

By the looks of things, Shouty Dad was close to exploding. He seemed to have quite a complicated plan about Shepherds and Wise Men and Camels and Disabled Sheep all walking slowly down different aisles and arriving at the stable at the same time, carrying presents and crooks and lambs and things. The problem was that the children would just wander off and get lost in the pews, or if they did turn up at the stable they were often empty-handed.

'Where's the frankincense?' Shouty Dad asked Little

William, who was wearing a 'Welcome to Swanage' souvenir tea towel on his head.

'The what?' Little William asked.

'Frankincense. It's one of the gifts for Baby Jesus. I gave it to you not THREE minutes ago and told you to keep it safe.'

Little William just shrugged. 'I don't have it,' he said.

So then there was a big search for the frankincense, which was loads of fun but we couldn't find it anywhere. Eventually they gave Little William a box of Maltesers to carry instead.

'Where are all the stable SHEEP?' Shouty Dad asked, hands on head.

'Oh, it's STABLE sheep!' I said. 'Not disabled sheep. That makes more sense.'

Harry was in place, as Joseph, standing behind Mary looking calm and reverent just as the real Joseph would have done. Then I realised he was playing on a 3DS which I'm sure the real Joseph wouldn't have done at such an anxious time.

'And where's the DONKEY?' Shouty Dad said, looking around.

'Mrs Bellamy took him for a wee,' Mary said then went back to chewing on the Baby Jesus's foot. Eventually everyone was on the stage. It looked a little crowded up there.

'What are you all EATING?' Shouty Dad shouted.

'Maltesers,' said the Archangel Gabriel.

Then it was time for William D's song and it didn't go well. There were three camels – William D, William P and Zach. Only Zach seemed to know the words and none of them danced.

'Come on boys,' Shouty Dad cried, exasperated. 'This is the big comic turn. You've got to bring the house down.'

William D just stood there looking like he was going to cry. The pressure was getting to all of us.

Later on I trudged into the school hall feeling exhausted. The last thing I wanted to do was have to deal with Imogen. As some of the teachers set out chairs for the audience and the stage crew tested the lights and the sound, Madame Adams called the cast together.

'This is the last performance,' she said. 'I know you're tired. You've done a fantastic job and you all deserve a good rest. But tonight, there's one more performance to do and it's being recorded. Let's make it the best one of all.'

We gave a cheer and I felt a bit better. Then Mr Bolli arrived, looking concerned and whispered something into Madame Adams' ear. Her eyes widened. When Mr Bolli had finished, she cleared her throat and frowned at us.

'I'm afraid we are without our Jasmine tonight. Imogen Downing is suffering from exhaustion and will not be able to be with us.'

Everyone gasped. I looked over at Thomas who looked at me and raised an eyebrow.

'This is a bit of a problem,' Madame Adams said,

'because Imogen's understudy, Georgie Brooks, is also ill. But do not worry,' she hastened to add when she saw our faces. 'I know the lines and I can play the part myself.'

Thomas's eyes widened in alarm. But then Mr Bolli cleared his throat. 'Unless . . .' he began but then paused.

'Yes Mr Bolli?' said Madame Adams.

'Well-a,' he began. 'Is there anyone else here who knows Jasmine's lines? One of the extras, or the stage crew, or minor characters? This-a could be your big big chance.'

There was complete silence as we all looked at each other. Emily hid behind Hannah. Tamsin climbed up a ladder. Tobias looked for a moment as if he was going to put up a hand, but didn't.

'OK,' Madame Adams sighed. 'Looks like I'll be Jasmine tonight.'

And then my wonderful little sister Daisy slowly raised her hand.

'Yes, Daisy?' Madame Adams said. 'What is it?'

'I know the lines,' Daisy replied in a tiny voice. 'I know all the lines.'

Madame Adams stepped towards her, her face full of sunshine. 'You would do it?' she asked. 'You'd be our Jasmine?'

'I probably wouldn't be very good,' Daisy said, her voice shaking a little.

'You'll be fabulous, darling.'

* * *

273

There wasn't time to tell Mummy what had happened, so I made sure I was watching through the wings when Daisy first came out on stage. I saw Mummy, right at the back, standing on a chair so she could see and ignoring Mrs Fuller who was asking her to get down. When Daisy came out, dressed as Jasmine, Mummy's eyes nearly popped out of their sockets. William D was right next to her looking bored until Mummy pointed out Daisy and then he got up on his chair too. And then the music started and the final performance began.

Daisy. Was. Brilliant.

She was miles better than Imogen. MILES. When Imogen was Jasmine the princess was all arrogant and superior. When Daisy was Jasmine the princess was sweet and funny. Even though they said the SAME LINES. The most brilliant thing of all was that without Imogen on stage I wasn't nervous any more. I had my Daisy with me, and it was just like when we practised in her bedroom. Emily was there too, and Tobias, and even Tamsin, halfway up a ladder, shining a light on us like she'd done with a torch from the top bunk.

The audience were fantastic too. When Emily said 'Quick, hide in here!' she got a laugh. And when I had to catch the snake I snatched it out of the air, spun around with a panicked face and hurled it deep into the audience, which got a huge laugh and shrieks. Thomas grinned like a Cheshire Cat.

The only thing I wasn't entirely happy about was the

romantic scene in the cave where the water is rising. Daisy didn't just hug Thomas. She KISSED him, on the cheek! It was only a little peck, but Thomas looked shocked and I think my jaw hit the floor. The audience loved it and a great 'Aaaaah!' echoed around the hall. Even Imogen hadn't had the nerve to kiss Thomas, but Daisy just carried on like it was no big deal. Even though I was a bit miffed I had to admire her professionalism.

But then I forgot about it because it was time for my monologue, which I absolutely NAILED. Even though Mr Bolli had told me to ignore the audience, I couldn't help but have a little peek towards the back as I stalked out onto stage. Mummy was up on her chair, booing loudly. William D joined in too. 'Boooo!' It was hard not to grin.

It was all over too soon and we left the stage and got big hugs from Mr Bolli and Madame Adams.

'A triumph,' she kept crying. 'A tour de force.'

As we got changed I grinned at Daisy and she grinned back at me, her face shining. She was bouncing with excitement. Somehow I think this won't be the last play she's ever in. Then Tobias raced in, leapt and slid across the floor of the classroom, crashing into a table and knocking it flying. Everyone laughed and clapped him on the back.

'You were amazing,' Mummy said on the way home. 'I am so proud of both of you.'

William D had found a tinfoil sword somewhere and

brought it home with him. He was swishing at the bedraggled nettles by the verge.

'It's a shame Daddy couldn't come,' I said.

'Don't worry,' Mummy said. 'I'll buy the DVD. He can watch it when he gets back from Germany.'

Lo, William D is Come

Friday evening was William D's big show. We were all exhausted after the excitement of the previous evening and it seemed odd that everything should just go back to being normal so quickly. We made it just in time, as Mummy had been working late again. It was OK though, because Mrs Bellamy had saved us all seats right near the front. She said loads of people were tutting at her because you weren't really allowed to save seats but she didn't care and just put a coat on a seat for each of us.

The show was brilliant, though not necessarily for all the right reasons. Shouty Dad had persisted with his plan about everyone making their way up to the stage from different directions. I could see the advantage of the plan. Usually what they do is bring all the children in down the central aisle, and it takes for ever. By the time all the children are crammed onto the little stage the intro music will have run out and there will be babies crying and toddlers escaping and the play will be behind schedule and everyone's ready to go home because they've been there an hour even before it started because otherwise you don't get a seat. But the way Shouty Dad had arranged it seemed like the children were just slipping in and all arriving together. We watched the Three Wise Men pass by us, carrying the presents. Or at least two of them had presents. It looked like they still hadn't found the frankincense.

Shouty Dad was shouting, but in a whispery sort of way. A stage shout, I suppose.

'What are you doing? It's not that way, it's this way. You're a sheep, not a shepherd! Well where has he gone NOW? Look, we rehearsed this!'

We could see William D arriving, in full camel costume, at the far side of the stage as Mary laid the chewed Baby Jesus in the manger. The three camels shuffled on and stood looking uncomfortable at the back of the stage, waiting for their big song. The cattle came in, a-lowing. They were followed by the disabled sheep and the shepherds. Harry didn't look beatific today. He looked bored without his 3DS. Everyone got on stage OK, though there was a brief squabble between two of the shepherds. Also one of the stars fell off the back of the stage and had a cry.

And so the children said their lines. Mostly you couldn't hear what they were saying because they just stared at their feet and mumbled, but Shynala was playing the Christmas Star and was narrating everything in a really loud voice so we could follow what was going on. Mummy tutted loudly at the lady in front who was filming on her iPad. Mary looked down at the Baby Jesus hungrily.

Finally it was time for the camel song. Mummy stood and started filming on her iPhone. People behind tutted loudly. The opening strains of the song began and we saw William D look up at us. Mummy waved and I gave him the thumbs up. I think he saw us. He grinned and launched into his song.

I've got the hump, I've been walking all day,
I've got the hump and I have to say,
I've got the hump, I've got the hump,
I've got the hump on Christmas Day.

I'm not sure what happened, maybe it was that we were all there, cheering him on, or maybe the Christmas spirit had got into him, but he really went for it. He was definitely the loudest of all the camels, he got most of the words right and hit some of the right notes. And the best thing of all was that he did his Mexican Dance as he sang and the whole church erupted with laughter. I could see he was pleased by the reaction and he carried on dancing even when the song had finished. Eventually he had to be dragged away by Mrs Duvall which got him another laugh and a cheer.

I turned to look at Mummy and she was wiping away tears she'd been laughing so much. This was just what she needed after such a stressful week.

Good old William D.

*   *   *

When we got home the builders were packing up. Mr Peterson said they were finished.

'Really?' I asked. 'All the work's done?'

'Yep,' Mummy said.

'Front Door is fixed?' Daisy asked.

'You betcha,' Mummy said.

So we had to go and check. Mummy was right, Front Door *was* fixed. You could open her and close her without any trouble, as often as you liked. We stood there, taking it in turns to stand outside, close the door and ring the bell, then someone else would open Front Door and let us in. Eventually Mummy yelled at us and told us to stop letting all the warm air escape.

I felt a bit sad about Front Door being fixed. It felt like her personality had been taken away, like there was now another member of the family missing. Daisy said we should call her New Front Door from now on.

Mummy got out a bottle of fizzy wine for the grown-ups to celebrate. We had lemonade and we all stood around admiring the wallpaper and the lovely new spindles. Mummy said that we had to stay out of some rooms because the paint was still drying. Mr Peterson was going to come back the next day and give us a proper tour. I was a bit sad when it was over and gave all the builders hugs as they left. Daisy cried a bit when she hugged Ana.

Ana knelt down and said, 'Goodbye, beautiful Jasmine.'

Piotr gave William D a hammer, which made Mummy frown a bit.

The Unknown Builder was the last to leave and he stopped on the way out of New Front Door and winked at me.

'Sophia Loren,' he said. Then he was gone.

Disaster

Mummy was super-cheerful when we got up on Saturday. It was two days until Christmas.

'All the plays are over. Yippee!' she said bouncing around the kitchen. 'Not that I didn't enjoy them all tremendously. And your father is back tonight for two whole weeks.'

'Yay!' we cried. 'Daddy's coming home.'

'And Mr Peterson's coming over today, to finish up a couple of things, then the decorating will be done.'

When Mr Peterson came he looked, if not happy, then at least not quite as sad as he usually did. He showed us all the building work they'd done.

'Look at all that,' he said pointing to the bricks over Front Door. 'Have you ever seen straighter brickwork?'

'No,' we replied dutifully, even though it looked the same to me.

He pulled up some floorboards on the first floor and pointed to the wooden beams underneath.

'Look,' he said. 'No damp.'

'Brilliant,' we said.

'What about the paintwork? The spindles?' he asked.

'Amazing,' we said.

And it was. Despite all the disruption, even though it had meant Daddy had had to go away so much, it was amazing. Our house looked brilliant. The best thing of all was all the new wallpaper on the first floor landing, which looked fantastic. Especially now you were able to turn on a light and see it. The haunted corridor seemed really bright and friendly.

Finally we ended up in my room. My real room, I mean. The attic.

'Wow,' said Mummy.

'Wow,' said Daisy.

'Wow,' said me.

It was beautiful. Ana had done a great job with the paintbrush and there were new curtains, the radiator had been replaced and it was warm and cosy.

'Can I move back in today, Mummy?' I asked.

She looked at me in surprise. 'I'd imagined this would be a spare room,' Mummy said. 'We're going to need all the room we can get when the Cooper-Deals arrive.'

'They can go in the Megadeath room,' I said firmly. 'I'm moving back in here.'

For a moment it looked like Mummy might argue, but then she shrugged and smiled. 'OK Chloe,' she said. 'Whatever you want.'

YES!

'Ooh, one more thing to show you,' Mr Peterson said. He led us down to the cellar.

'We had to rewire most of the house,' he said. 'The old fusebox wasn't up to code so we replaced it with the most up-to-date circuit control system available. Here it is.' He indicated what looked like a computer screen, surrounded by buttons, lights, wires and a little keypad.

'It looks complicated,' Mummy said.

'Not complicated at all,' Mr Peterson said. 'It's all very straightforward. It works just like an iPhone – touch-screen technology, all very user-friendly. You can't go wrong.'

Mummy nodded and shrugged and we all went back upstairs into the kitchen where Mummy gave Mr Peterson a mince pie and a cup of tea and he even smiled.

'This is going to be a brilliant Christmas,' Daisy said.

As if in reply, the door to the garden shivered in its frame. Wind was sweeping through the garden. Mr Peterson turned to look outside and frowned.

'There's a storm coming,' he said.

And Mr Peterson was right. The wind just got worse and worse over the next few hours. It came howling from the east, dumping rain and hail that battered the windows and the roof. The trees bent in the garden and the cats huddled together next to the Aga. But we were safe and cosy warm in our house.

Around four o'clock the phone rang. It was Daddy.

'The whole airport's closed?' Mummy said. 'But it's in Germany. Things don't shut down in Germany.'

But it turns out they do. Daddy said he was going to

try and get on a train and get to France but that he thought the ferries might be stuck in port until the storm ended. Well, we were all very glum after that. The idea that Daddy might not be home for Christmas was something we didn't really want to think about.

'He's got a large ham, some German sausage and a bottle of schnapps,' Mummy said, reading his text. 'So at least he's not going to starve.'

On the news there were lots of reports about how no one could get to anywhere because of the storms all across Europe. No planes were flying and there were hardly any ferries.

'And the Cooper-Deals are arriving first thing tomorrow morning,' Mummy said.

I went to bed that night excited about being back in my proper room, Christmas and about the Cooper-Deals coming, but worried about Daddy. It took me a long time to go to sleep, with all the howling of the wind and the creaking of the house. I crept downstairs at one point and found Mummy asleep on the sofa in front of a film. I turned off the telly and put a blanket over her before going back up to bed.

They're Here!

The Cooper-Deals arrived super-early on Christmas Eve. The wind was still very strong and Daddy was still not home. Mummy said he was in Holland now, which is in the right direction but still on the wrong side of the North Sea. New Front Door rang and William D got there first. Uncle Desmond was standing there, swaying in the wind and holding up a huge box of Christmas lights.

'Can't believe you don't have any lights up,' he said coming in and bringing a gallon of rain water with him. 'Luckily I bought these in the January sales last year. You get them for nothing just after Christmas, nothing.'

'Ooh, it's lovely,' said Auntie Moira coming in and looking around.

Uncle Ryan charged in, shoving William D aside, and ran upstairs like he owned the place. William D grabbed a walking stick as a weapon from the rack near New Front Door and raced up after his uncle. Then came Grandpa Jim, helped up the steps by Auntie Lisa. Brittany followed and Natasha brought up the rear, looking pale, and asking if Jacob was around.

'Hi Brittany,' I said. 'Come upstairs and see my room.'

'Then come and see my room,' Daisy said.

'Which of your rooms is bigger?' Brittany asked as we went up the stairs.

'Mine is,' Daisy said.

I frowned. 'Mine has a nicer view though,' I said.

'I don't think so,' Daisy said.

There was a terrific crash from upstairs and we rushed into William D's room to find Uncle Ryan had pulled everything out of the toy cupboard and scattered it all over the floor. The boys were fighting over a toy truck that I knew for a fact William D hadn't played with for over a year.

The place already looked like a bomb had hit it.

Within an hour or so the whole *house* looked like a bomb had hit it. It had all been so neat and tidy yesterday, before the storm. Now the corridors were full of people and noise. Bags and presents and coats and jumpers were scattered all over the place. Uncle Desmond was outside stringing up row after row of lights. I went out to watch him and hold the stepladder, which had been swaying alarmingly in the wind.

'You'll be the brightest house on the street,' he called down to me.

'Great,' I called back.

Mummy was slightly frazzled, but I think it helped us having lots of people around. It took our minds off worrying about Daddy. She'd had a text from him around 9 a.m. saying he was still in Holland but his phone battery was running low so he was going to turn it off.

Mummy told me to come in after a bit because I was soaked and shivering. She wrapped a towel around me and I went into the kitchen to warm up next to the Aga. Auntie Moira was busy making cup after cup of tea. William D was scribbling on a piece of paper at the kitchen table. When he concentrates he sticks his tongue out a bit. Grandpa Jim watched him as he ran out of space on the paper to scribble on and moved on to the table. Jacob came in, followed by Natasha. Jacob was checking his phone mournfully every five minutes. I glared at him but he ignored me.

'So where is John now?' Grandpa Jim asked for the hundredth time.

'He'll be here,' Mummy said, gritting her teeth. 'He'll be here.'

In the afternoon we went for a walk around town, just to get out of the house for a bit. It was so cold and windy! All the Christmas lights in town were swaying. Litter flew down the street and even though the rain wasn't heavy, it stung your face and seemed to creep inside your rain coat. We all squashed into the Olive Tree café for hot chocolate, and to warm up. And before we knew it, it was dark again and everyone was getting hungry so we headed home, cold and wet but excited and chatting nineteen to the dozen. The only problem was that Daddy wasn't there. I could see Mummy checking her phone all the time.

In Germany, they have their big celebration on Christmas Eve rather than Christmas Day, and Mummy had gone for a German theme for supper. There was black bread, sausage, ham and Black Forest gâteau. Mummy had got everything from Lidl. The idea had been that we'd be welcoming Daddy back with a surprise German supper.

Moira insisted on helping Mummy prepare the meal, which involved always standing exactly where Mummy needed to be and picking up utensils and jamming them into the dishwasher a few seconds before Mummy needed them again. Apart from that, she mostly stood holding a glass of wine, talking about how much she loved the house and how lovely the decorating was but also how she would have done it slightly differently.

Mummy just grunted as her ears went white and her cheeks went red. The wind was still howling outside and I heard a tapping on the door. Clematis stood outside with a little creature in his jaws. I couldn't tell what sort of animal it was but it didn't look like one we'd had before. I think Mummy must have locked the cat flap to stop him coming in.

Mummy rushed over to the door and growled through the glass. 'Go away, you horrible cat,' she shouted.

Clematis just looked up at her as the creature struggled weakly in his jaws. I left the kitchen before Mummy exploded and went to see what the others were doing. In the playroom, Grandpa Jim was watching an episode of Pokémon Black and White with Uncle Ryan and William D, who was running a quiz at the same time.

'What is Zorith the Fog Creature's favourite colour,' William D asked. 'A) Blue B) Red C) Black?'

'Err, black?' Grandpa Jim replied.

'That's right!' William D said. He looked up at me and mouthed the word 'wrong' while rolling his eyes and shaking his head. 'Well done, Grandpa,' he said.

Grandpa Jim looked pleased. There was a howling gale in the sitting room. Auntie Lisa had the window open and her head stuck out, shouting at Uncle Desmond who had decided there still weren't quite enough lights out the front of the house. I could see she had a new tattoo on her lower back. I think it was Harry Styles' face but it might have been Medusa.

'Get down, you silly fool,' she yelled. 'You'll kill yourself.'

'Just this last string,' Uncle Desmond cried. 'Then we're done.'

I wandered upstairs to find Daisy and Brittany. They were sitting in Daisy's room. Brittany was braiding Daisy's hair.

'Whose doll is that?' Brittany asked me, nodding towards Dirty Millie.

I stiffened. The ownership of Dirty Millie has been a long running dispute between me and Daisy. We don't argue about much, but neither of us will accept that the other might have any claim on the doll. Dirty Millie is a big old rag doll with straggly hair and a big stain on her pinafore. She used to be Mummy's and Daisy and I have an uneasy agreement in which we share her. This shows that I'm the bigger person because really Dirty Millie is mine. Trust Brittany to find the one thing that might drive a wedge between me and Daisy.

'We share her,' I said stiffly even though what I wanted to say was 'SHE'S MINE!'

I expected Daisy to also say 'we share her'. But she didn't.

'She's mine,' Daisy said. My jaw dropped. 'But I let Chloe play with her sometimes.'

Well, I'm sorry to say there was an incident between me and Daisy. Mummy was not happy about having to come upstairs and drag us apart. She told me I had to keep away from my sister for an hour and she confiscated Dirty Millie altogether which earned me another furious look from Daisy. As I was hauled out of the room, I saw Brittany lying innocently on the daybed reading a Harry Potter book.

Despite Mummy checking her phone every five minutes, there was still no sign of Daddy. I checked my phone too in case he'd got the numbers mixed up but there was nothing. The last we'd heard from him he'd been on a coach heading towards Boulogne in France, where the Eurotunnel terminal is. But he'd said there were long queues for the trains and it wasn't likely he'd be able to get a seat tonight. That had been hours ago and we were worried sick about him.

New Front Door rang so I raced downstairs and for once got there first. I opened the door, hoping to see Daddy, and was disappointed to see Mr Coleman carrying Clematis. He handed the cat to me as Mummy came up behind me.

'Hello Mr Coleman,' Mummy said.

'He came into my house, carrying a dead animal,' Mr Coleman said.

'Thank you,' I said, wondering if I could ask Mr Coleman what he'd done with the creature and whether he could maybe take a picture for me so I could identify it officially.

'I'm going away tonight,' he said. 'And won't be back until the New Year. I'm looking forward to some peace and quiet. Could you please make sure your cat stays out of my house, because I really don't want to come home after Christmas to find dead animals all over the place.'

'Yes, of course,' Mummy said. 'Totally understand.'

'Good,' Mr Coleman said rudely, before turning and walking off into the gale.

'Merry Christmas!' Mummy called after him.

Mummy had pulled out the big table in the study/

playroom and put away William D's toys. When we walked in I had to stop and rub my eyes in amazement. The room had been transformed. There were decorations hanging from the light fittings. There were holly wreaths and twig bundles tied with gold ribbon. Mummy had also brought through her tasteful small tree with just a few bows and some white lights. But it was the table itself which was the most amazing thing. It was creaking under the weight of the food on it. There was black bread, sausages, a selection of sauces and creams, three different potato dishes, a ham, cold chicken, bean salad and green salad, crackers and cheese, grapes and on the sideboard was a massive Black Forest gâteau. Jacob loaded his plate high with just about everything but he blanched when he smelled the pickled eggs.

'Eugh, vinegar,' he said.

Everyone grabbed a plate and tucked in. For once, we were allowed to eat in the sitting room. William D and Uncle Ryan kept forgetting to put anything in their mouths because they were staring at the mountain of presents under the tree. Jacob had found himself squashed in next to Natasha on the sofa. Natasha wasn't wearing quite as much as she could have been, in my opinion. And from where I was sitting it actually looked like there was enough room that it wasn't quite necessary for her to be almost sitting on top of Jacob like that. We all pulled crackers and told the jokes. Everyone was talking and arguing and laughing and singing. Everyone except

Mummy, who kept looking at New Front Door. I caught her eye at one point and smiled. She smiled back, but I could tell she was worried.

So was I.

New Front Door rang again around 8 p.m.

'Daddy!' we all cried. And again we raced to open her.

It wasn't Daddy this time either. But it was nearly as good.

'CHARLIE!' we all screamed.

And there she was, back from Africa with a bagful of presents, grinning and browner than German bread. I gave her a massive hug and had a quick sniff to make sure there was no smell of vinegar. There wasn't! We dragged her into the sitting room and made introductions which took ages because there were so many of us.

'I don't want to impose,' she said, but Mummy said, 'You must stay and eat with us. One more won't make a difference.'

'Hello Jacob,' Charlie said.

We all looked over at him, still squashed under Natasha who was looking Charlie up and down like Clematis does to Mr Campbell's dog, Albert.

'Don't get up.'

'Hello Charlie,' Jacob said. 'I can't get up actually. I'm a bit squashed in here.'

'You look quite comfortable to me,' Charlie said.

'Comfortable isn't quite the word I'd choose,' he said. 'Excuse me Natasha, could you please let me out?'

Natasha sighed and shifted to let him go. He got up stiffly and went to help Charlie get some food in the next room. William D, Uncle Ryan, Daisy, Emily, Brittany and I all tried to follow but Mummy and Auntie Lisa blocked our path. There was a moment's silence as everyone waited to see what would happen next. We heard Charlie squeal from the dining room.

'OOH, pickled eggs!'

The Night Before Christmas
A short play by Chloe Deal

Int: Night. Christmas Eve. Empty plates and glasses litter the stage. All cast except for Daddy are present. There is carousing. Jacob and Charlie sit together. Jacob is shaking his head in disappointment as Charlie bites into a large pickled egg. Natasha is sitting on the other side of the room, glaring at Charlie.

Desmond: Time for the main event!

Children: (chorus) What main event?

Desmond: Switching on the Christmas lights, of course.

Cast exit stage left.

Ext: Front of house. Night. Cast huddling against wind and rain. And sleet. Dramatic music. Desmond is fiddling with light cable.

SFX: Howling wind sound. Complaining children.

Moira: Get on with it!

Desmond: Give us a chance! Got a great

deal on these lights. Less than half
price. Only problem is they're from
Kazakhstan and they have different
electrics there so I need an adaptor.
Uncle Ryan: I can't feel my toes.
Desmond: (fitting plug into adaptor)
Right, that's got it. Let's have a
countdown!
All: (chorus) 10 . . . 9 . . . 8 . . .
7 . . .
FX: Lightning flashes in sky.
All: (chorus) . . . 6 . . . 5 . . .
4 . . . 3 . . . 2 . . . 1
SFX: Music reaches climax.
Desmond: Go!
Desmond plugs in lights.
*FX: All floodlights come on, lighting
stage brilliantly.*
All: (chorus) Oooh!
FX: Loud bang off stage. Lights go out.
William D: Awkward.

I shone the torch on the new fusebox as Desmond and Grandpa Jim stared at it in confusion. Desmond tapped the screen and a flashing red message popped up saying: E30187YK – System Error. Please contact Vendor.

'It's all computers,' Desmond said. 'Where's the trip switch?'

'How is it even working if we don't have electricity?' Grandpa Jim said. He stepped forward to have a closer look but then suddenly was down on the floor with a thump.

'Ow,' he said. 'I tripped. Ooh, me ankle.'

'Get Jacob,' Desmond said to me.

I ran upstairs and told Jacob to come and help. Together Desmond and Jacob helped Grandpa Jim back up the stairs and into the sitting room where Mummy, Moira and Auntie Lisa were lighting dozens of candles. The fire was blazing bright and warm.

'Oh Jim, what have you done?' Auntie Lisa said, hugging him.

'I'd better go back down and see if I can figure out how the fusebox works,' Uncle Desmond said.

'Leave it,' Mummy said. 'We don't want any more injuries. The gas heating is still on so we won't freeze. And we have the fire, candles and torches. We'll sort it out in the morning.'

I saw her look again at New Front Door. I knew she was hoping Daddy would appear at any moment and save the day. But this time New Front Door stayed silent.

'Alone in the house, Melissa sat with a blanket around her shoulders, waiting for the storm to end . . .' Auntie Lisa told the story slowly, in her slightly raspy voice.

Outside, just like in the story, the storm shrieked and regular flashes of lightning darted behind the curtains. Rain lashed the window and wind rattled the frames. But inside, firelight flickered cheery orange and the room was toasty warm. We huddled together, looking into the fire and telling ghost stories. William D and Uncle Ryan were in bed. Mummy sat on an armchair, with Daisy snuggled on her lap. Uncle Desmond was sitting on a dining room chair next to them. Brittany and I were on the rug right next to the fire, stroking Clematis and The Slug who had crept in for the warmth. Behind us on the sofa were Auntie Moira, Natasha, Jacob and Charlie. Grandpa Jim sat on the other armchair with his injured foot up and Auntie Lisa perched on the arm as she told the story.

It was extremely crowded.

'Lightning flashed outside and the rain came down,' she continued. 'As the wind rose up, an old tree branch started knocking against the side of the house. Bang . . . bang . . . bang.'

I shivered as Auntie Lisa went on, and shifted Clematis

onto my lap so I'd have something to hang on to. He purred and rolled over onto his back, snuggling his furry face into my tummy.

'Melissa checked her phone again, but there was no battery left. Where was Jack? He should have been back from the store hours ago. Eventually, she dropped off to sleep, but the banging of the tree branch woke her up again. Bang . . . bang . . . bang.'

I turned my head to look up at Jacob and noticed Natasha shifting over towards him. He'd moved away, closer to Charlie, who was raising an eyebrow at all this movement.

'. . . But something was different this time. It took a moment for Melissa to realise what it was. Then it hit her. The banging sound wasn't coming from the *side* of the house any more. The wind had dropped. It wasn't a tree branch she could hear at all. Melissa stood and turned towards the direction the sound was coming from. Bang, bang, bang . . . And then her heart nearly stopped. Her breath caught in her throat and she froze to the spot as she realised that the sound was coming from . . .'

BANG! BANG! BANG!

'Aaagh!' I screamed.

'Aaagh!' screamed everyone else.

I clutched Clematis like a lifeline and he sank his claws into my arm. I shrieked again. How had Auntie Lisa made that noise? She hadn't moved.

'It's the door,' Mummy called over the hubbub. 'There's someone at the door!'

Jacob squeezed out from between Natasha and Charlie and rushed for the door, grabbing a torch on the way. I followed, Daisy right behind me. Jacob opened New Front Door and we gasped. On the doorstep towered a huge, dark figure carrying a club. A killer! Rain and sleet whipped past him into the house, stinging our eyes. The shadowy figure stepped forward, coming for us. Daisy screamed and maybe I did too. Jacob flicked on the torch and shone it into the killer's face.

'Daddy!' we cried.

Daddy stumbled into the house and sank to his knees. He dropped the 'club' he'd been carrying, which turned out to be an enormous ham. Just like Sophia Loren in *La Mortadella*. We gave him the biggest hug ever, even though he was wet and smelled of damp and cured meat.

'I'm here,' he muttered, squeezing me tight.

It turned out Daddy had hitched a ride with a truck driver in Boulogne who'd let him ride on his lorry through the Eurotunnel.

'I gave him the sausage to say thanks,' Daddy said.

'And did he drive you all the way here?' Mummy asked.

'No, I got a train to London,' Daddy said. 'But the Weyford trains were all cancelled because of the storm. I managed to get on a coach going to Guildford and persuaded the driver to make a little detour.'

'How did you persuade him?' I asked.

'I gave him the bottle of schnapps,' Daddy said. 'So all I have left is the ham.'

'It's a lovely ham,' Mummy said, admiring it.

'How much did you pay for that, then?' Uncle Desmond asked. Auntie Moira elbowed him in the tummy.

'Oh, I do have one more thing,' Daddy said, reaching into his bag. He pulled out a square parcel and showed us.

'A PlayBox IV!' Daisy and I squealed.

'I hope William D has filled his Mega Star Chart?' Daddy asked.

'Not even close,' Mummy said. 'But don't worry. We'll think of something.'

'Why are the lights off?' Daddy said. 'Is it a power cut?'

Mummy explained about the Christmas lights and the New Fuse Box and how we were going to sort it out in the morning. Daddy shrugged and said he liked it better with just the fire and the candles. So Daddy squeezed on to the sofa between me and Daisy. Clematis came back in and jumped on his chest for a snooze. Auntie Lisa finished her story but it wasn't scary any more. Not now I had Daddy back.

'Do you think you'll go back to Germany after Christmas?' I asked him.

He thought for a moment. 'Do you know, Chloe, I

must say when it comes to Europe, the novelty's worn off a bit. It's true that they make nice sausages there and they all carry handkerchiefs. But all in all, home's best, really. Home's best.'

Mummy woke me up just before midnight. I'd dropped off with my head on Daddy's chest. The other children had already gone up to bed. She gave me a torch and told me to brush my teeth before I got into bed. As I walked through the hall towards the staircase I felt a cold draft and noticed that New Front Door was slightly ajar. Worried that it had broken already. I walked towards it and heard a noise outside. I peeped around the doorway and saw two figures standing on the stoop, kissing underneath the mistletoe.

Now, I know I shouldn't have done it. I know they wanted some privacy. But I had to know who the girl was. Jacob had been getting texts from Taffeta, Natasha had been following him around like a lovesick puppy. And Charlie had been eating pickled eggs.

So I flicked on the torch and shone it right at them. They broke off and squinted at me in annoyance.

'Goodnight Jacob,' I said, giggling. 'Goodnight Charlie!'

Tangerines

We had one more visitor in the night.

'SANTA'S BEEN!' William screamed, charging into my room and waking me up. He was holding a BattleMaster toy in one hand and a tangerine in the other.

'Did he bring you some good presents?' I asked, sleepily.

'Yeah,' he said. 'But what's this all about?' he said, showing me the tangerine. He rushed out again to go and make sure no one in the house was left asleep. I sat up in bed and blinked to focus on my alarm clock. It was 5.22 a.m. That's a lie-in by William D's festive standards.

My stocking lay at the end of my bed, invitingly full, but I didn't pick it up just yet. Instead I walked to the window and looked out over the peaceful street. My room was warm enough now that I didn't even need to put my slippers on. The new boiler was doing its job. The storm had ended and a half moon gave the rooftops opposite a silvery glow that almost made it look like it had been snowing. I sighed happily as I thought of the day ahead.

First we'd have a noisy breakfast all together. William D would probably eat too fast and get the hiccups. Mummy would make Daddy laugh so much milk would come out of his nose. Auntie Lisa would tell us Christmas stories. Then the little children would be desperate to open all their presents and the grown-ups would take their time and say 'what's the hurry?' and the older children would pretend to be patient and Jacob wouldn't be up yet and I'd have to go and knock on his door and get him to come down and have breakfast before we could start the unwrapping.

Then we'd all squeeze into the sitting room and there'd be a blizzard of Christmas paper and Auntie Moira would try to tidy up as we went and she'd bring through bin liners we could put the scrap paper in and Grandpa Jim would take ages just to open his first present which would be a book which he'd start reading straight away even before he'd opened any other presents and Daddy would get socks and beer and a box of Ferrero Rocher which we'd all end up eating. Mummy would get perfume or a handbag or maybe an electric carving knife that she wouldn't be happy with.

Then we'd play with our new toys until lunch, which would be about an hour late, and William D and Uncle Ryan would be grumbling about being hungry and Auntie Moira would tell them they should have eaten more at breakfast and why not have a tangerine?

Then eventually Christmas dinner would be ready and

the table would be piled high with food. I'd be so hungry I'd want to eat it all but when I'd scoffed down a huge plateful of turkey and ham and crispy roast potatoes and sweet carrots and pigs in blankets and stuffing and gravy and bread sauce and forced down some Brussels sprouts and everyone else had done the same there'd still seem to be just as much food on the table as before.

After dinner Mummy and Auntie Moira and Auntie Lisa would want to go out for a walk and the men would want to have a snooze and the children would want to play with our new toys and Jacob would want to go to Charlie's house to give her her present and there'd be a big row and we'd agree to watch the Queen's speech first and the men would be asleep by the end of it and the mummies would drag us out for a quick walk around the park but it would start to rain and we'd come home, cheeks red and toes cold and get back to playing with our presents.

And in the evening we'd have cold turkey and ham and hot oven chips and we'd all watch a film together and the grown-ups would drink wine and we'd be allowed to have lemonade and William D and Ryan would be flopping about all over the place, exhausted and punching each other because they'd got up so early. And I'd never want it to end, but I'd be tired myself. Tired in a happy way. Happy that my family was around me on Christmas Day.

In some ways it was going to be a really long day but

at the same time it was going to be over in a flash. It hadn't quite started yet and I wanted to stretch this moment out as long as I could. My breath frosted the glass as I peered out, up and down the quiet, dark street. Quiet and dark, that is, until I saw a light flick on across the road, in Shouty Dad's house.

'IT'S NOT EVEN FIVE-THIRTY! GO BACK TO BED!'

However long this day was going to be, it was going to seem even longer for poor old Shouty Dad.

Everything turned out just as I'd imagined except for two things.

Firstly, there was a mad terrible panic in the morning when Mummy realised she didn't have any foil for the turkey.

'That was the one thing they'd run out of at LIDL,' she wailed. 'I was going to pop into Sainsbury's but I forgot.'

The Bellamys weren't at home, neither were Mr Coleman or Gavin and Justin from next door the other way.

Mummy took a deep breath. 'Oh god,' she said. 'I'm going to have to go and knock on doors up and down the street on Christmas morning.'

But just as she was pulling on her coat, Uncle Ryan raced past, screaming and pursued by William D who was taking swipes at him with the sword he'd brought back from the play.

Mummy's jaw dropped. 'Stop him, Chloe. Stop him!'

Surprised, but always ready to spring into action, I dived as William D passed and tackled him to the ground. Mummy stepped up and wrenched the sword from his fingers as he roared in protest. She held it up to me.

'Don't you see, Chloe?' she said, her eyes shining. 'Don't you see?'

'See what?' I asked. But then I realised what she was on about. William D's sword was made of . . . Bacofoil!

We rushed it into the kitchen and unwrapped it carefully, smoothing it out into a sheet. There was just enough. William D stomped in behind us looking furious.

'William D,' Mummy said, kneeling down and looking into his eyes. 'Do you know what you just did?'

'What?' he asked grumpily.

'You just saved Christmas,' Mummy said. And she grabbed the packet of stickers from the top of the fridge, peeled the back off an entire sheet and slapped it right onto the middle of William D's star chart. His eyes lit up.

'Does this mean I can have . . .'

'. . . Yes it does,' Mummy said. She reached up on top of the fridge, brought down the PlayBox IV and gave it to William D then and there.

I have never before seen such a delightedly flabbergasted face.

'You are amazing,' William D said breathlessly, looking up at Mummy.

'I know,' she said.

The other thing that happened slightly differently to my prediction occured when we were opening our presents. William D likes to be in charge of the sorting and he tends to pile everyone's presents up in front of them. When he'd sorted all the presents, Brittany peered over and said, 'Daisy, why is your pile bigger than Chloe's?'

'It isn't,' she said.

But it was. I knew it didn't really matter. The size of the pile wasn't the important thing. I hadn't asked for much really, except for the return of Daddy. But Brittany wouldn't let it go. She left her own pile and came over and started to count our presents. But Daisy put her hand on Brittany's arm to stop her.

'It doesn't matter who has the biggest pile,' Daisy said. 'Chloe and I always share everything anyway.' She looked up at me and we grinned at each other.

'Even Dirty Millie?' Brittany asked innocently.

'Even Dirty Millie,' Daisy said.

'*Especially* Dirty Millie,' I added.

Brittany scowled and went back to her own presents.

William D looked up from his presents and stood, torn Christmas paper falling away from him. A look of delirious joy washed over his face. Then he launched himself at Ryan, expressing his festive spirit through an unprovoked attack on his uncle.

'BATTLEMASTER!!!!' he screamed.

On the Twelfth Day of Christmas My Black Cat Brought to Me:

Twelve tiny mouslings
Eleven butterflies
Ten buzzing wasps
Nine headless voles
Eight mangled sparrows
Seven chewed blackbirds
Six disembowelled pigeons
Five torn-off wings
Four bloody shrews
Three legless robins
Two baby birds
And a squirrel that wasn't quite dead.

Piccadilly
P R E S S

Thank you for choosing a Piccadilly Press book.

If you would like to know more about our authors, our books or if you'd just like to know what we're up to, you can find us online.

www.piccadillypress.co.uk

You can also find us on:

We hope to see you soon!